DO
NOT
PASS
GO

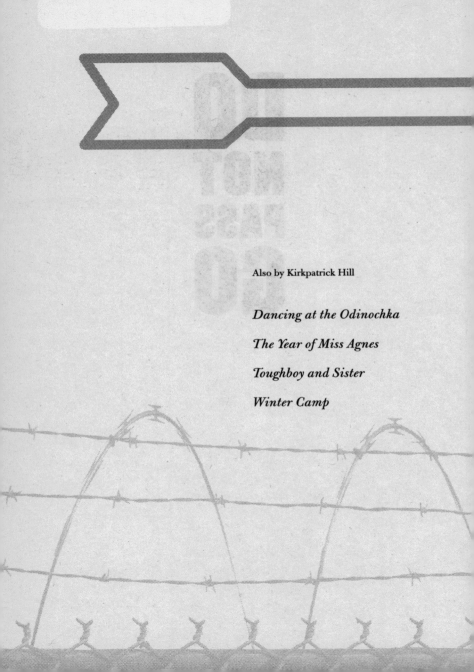

DO NOT PASS GO

KIRKPATRICK HILL

Margaret K. McElderry Books New York London Toronto Sydney

MARGARET K. McELDERRY BOOKS
An imprint of Simon & Schuster Children's Publishing Division
1230 Avenue of the Americas, New York, New York 10020
This book is a work of fiction. Any references to historical events, real
people, or real locales are used fictitiously. Other names, characters,
places, and incidents are products of the author's imagination, and any
resemblance to actual events or locales or persons, living or dead, is
entirely coincidental.

For information about special discounts for bulk purchases, please
contact Simon & Schuster Special Sales at 1-866-506-1949 or
business@simonandschuster.com.
The Simon & Schuster Speakers Bureau can bring authors to your live
event. For more information or to book an event, contact the Simon &
Schuster Speakers Bureau at 1-866-248-3049 or visit our website at
www.simonspeakers.com.
Also available in a Margaret K. McElderry Books hardcover edition
The text for this book is set in Bulmer.
Manufactured in the United States of America
0611 OFF
First Margaret K. McElderry Books paperback edition July 2011
10 9 8 7 6 5 4 3 2 1
The Library of Congress has cataloged the hardcover edition as follows:
Hill, Kirkpatrick.
Do not pass go / Kirkpatrick Hill.—1st ed.
p. cm.
Summary: When Deet's father is jailed for using drugs, Deet learns that
prison is not what he expected, nor are other people necessarily the way
he thought they were.
ISBN 978-1-4169-1400-6 (hc)
[1. Prisoners—Fiction. 2. Fathers—Fiction. 3. Family life—Alaska—
Fiction. 4. Interpersonal relations—Fiction. 5. Quotations—Fiction.
6. Alaska—Fiction.] I. Title.
PZ7.H55285Do 2007
[Fic]—dc22
2006003254
ISBN 978-1-4424-2122-6 (pbk)
ISBN 978-1-4391-0412-5 (eBook)

FOR SEAN

Merry-hearted boys make the best of old men.

—The Bard of Armagh

ONE

Deet tenderly wiped the drips

of new oil from the engine of the Mercedes and replaced the dipstick. The engine was spotless and elegant-looking, like the car. He used a clean corner of the rag to polish the carburetor cover before he shut the hood, which closed with a wonderful oiled *snick*. The Mercedes had California plates, not Alaska plates.

"How come they brought this car in *here*?" Deet asked.

Deet's dad scooted his creeper out a little from under the car to look up at him, his eyebrows raised in pretend indignation. "What do you mean, in *here*, like it was a black hole or something?"

Deet gave him a severe look. "You know what I mean. This is not a Mercedes kind of garage, it's a truck kind of garage. *Old* trucks."

Deet's dad laughed and with a quick lurch scooted the creeper backward to grab a wrench from a pile of tools behind him.

"Yeah, well. This car belongs to an old friend of Dan's from California. Otherwise it probably *would* have been taken someplace else." He patted the silver door with appreciation. "Sweet, isn't she." He disappeared under the car again.

Deet thought Dan's Garage looked like the set for a fifties movie starring someone like John Travolta. Except for the gas pumps, which were very modern and didn't look right with the white cement-block building.

There was a pyramid of dusty oilcans in the dirty front window, and piles of dog-eared and greasy parts manuals sat on the counter next to an old cash register. There was a candy bar machine by the doorway leading to the shop.

Various dingy display items were tacked up on the beaverboard walls—plastic windshield scrapers, keychains with tiny flashlights on them, and green felt pine trees to make your car smell better. The pine trees had been there so long the smell had gone out of them.

Dan was the old guy who owned the garage, had owned it since he was young. He was really mellow, with all this wild white hair stuck under a duck-bill cap.

As far as Deet knew, only one thing made Dan mad, and that was bumper stickers, and the kinds of slogans people stuck all over their cars. "I don't want to know your politics, I don't want to know your religion, and I don't want to know what you do for a hobby!" he'd snarl at an offending car parked in one of the bays. Deet's dad said if a car came in with too many stickers, Dan would refuse to work on it. "Too busy, got 'em stacked up," he'd say, barely civil.

One of the other mechanics, Willy, had been at the garage with old Dan since the beginning. You could see yourself on the top of Willy's head, he was so cleanly bald. And then there was Deet's dad, Charley Aafedt, and Bingo. Bingo the Bulk, Dan called him, because he was so big. Bingo and Deet's dad had been there more than twelve years, so it wasn't a place with a lot of turnover, except for the tire guys. The tire guys, mostly kids just out of high school, came and went pretty regularly, on their way to better jobs with a little experience under their belts.

Gary was the new tire guy this winter, and he was a little older than most tire guys were, kind of beat-up–looking, but he was a ball of fire, loud and funny and full of energy. Deet didn't get to see much of him, because Gary only worked in the mornings.

Deet had been coming in to help since he was a little kid, since his mom had married Charley, and in that time nothing had ever changed in the garage. There was a grimy girlie calendar over the workbench that had been there, opened to the same month, for as long as he could remember. None of the guys were the naked-girl-calendar type and yet it hung there, year after year. When Deet asked Dan one day why he never took it down. Dan looked up fondly at the naked lady and said, "Because they don't make calendars like that anymore." Whatever that meant.

All the guys had taught Deet a little of this and that. Even though he wasn't old enough for a driver's license, they let him drive the cars that were finished out of the bay and out to the back to wait for the customers. They let him change the oil, put on new wiper blades, check the radiators. And they called him to watch when something interesting was going on—a tricky transmission job, a creative radiator patch.

Deet was good at mechanical stuff, but it couldn't be said that he really liked working on cars. He was glad to know how the engines worked, the way he was glad to know everything, but it wasn't what he had in mind for himself. He wanted to be a scientist. Or do some kind of work that lasted, that you didn't have to do over again in a few months.

Deet picked up the used oilcans and took them to the trash bin. He washed his hands in the chipped sink, then went over to the corner by a pile of old tires and made a sort of chair for himself with two tires under him and one behind his back. He always put his book bag there when he came in, and when he was finished helping the guys, he'd start his homework.

Mr. Hodges had given them all paperback quotation books in English class today. He had written the first quotation on the board:

It's a good thing for an uneducated man to read books of quotations.—Winston Churchill

Of course Mr. Hodges had to take a lot of flak from the girls about the word man, and then some more about calling the kids in the class uneducated, because what had they been spending all these years doing, anyway, if it wasn't getting an education, but it was all very good-natured. Everyone liked Mr. Hodges, who jittered around like a terrier, clutching what was left of the hair over his ears in mock despair over their questions and answers.

The quotation book was divided into subjects. You could find a quotation about almost anything. Every week they were supposed to pick out two they liked and write short essays about what they thought the quotations meant, and this would take the place of their regular Thursday homework on vocabulary. Deet thought this was going to be very interesting, like everything Mr. Hodges had them do.

He looked up "mechanics" first, to see if there was anything that applied to the guys in the shop. Nothing. That was strange. Millions of mechanics all over the world, keeping everything running, and nobody had a quote about them? Talk about the unsung hero.

Deet looked up at Bingo and Willy, working in the bays. Born mechanics, that's what people like them were called. If a kid was born two hundred years ago, you couldn't have said he was a born mechanic, because that hadn't been thought of yet. What was there before mechanics? Maybe a kid like that would be interested in wagons, or horses. No, horses would be a whole different thing. Maybe cotton gins and spinning wheels. Deet wasn't quite sure what either of those things were, but it sounded like they had moving parts.

Deet flipped through the quotation book, looking for inspiration. Every category in the world besides mechanics: birds, causes and consequences, knowledge, liberty, love, education. Buying and selling.

Socrates, walking in the marketplace, had said:

How much there is in the world I do not want.

He could just see Socrates in that white sheet thing—toga in Rome, but he forgot what it was called in Greece—walking in his sandals, walking with his students. What kind of thing would the Greeks be selling that Socrates had no use for? Deet wasn't sure. He opened his notebook and wrote the quotation down at the top of the page in his small, precise printing, all the lowercase letters just the same size, each word spaced the same as the others. Then he looked up Socrates in his dictionary. 470-399 B.C. Under the quotation he wrote:

Socrates wrote this twenty-four hundred years ago, and I feel like this every time I go through the mall and look at all the junk there is to buy. Like phony diamond lizard key chains, and cookie jars shaped like Elvis, and lamp bases that bubble colored oil or something. To think of people spending their lives in factories making this junk. How could you have job satisfaction doing something like that? I used to like those books about pioneer days, the people in houses they made themselves, with just what they needed around them. Just enough furniture, and a quilt made of goose feathers, and carefully carved shelves, and when they needed something they couldn't make themselves they'd sell their butter or eggs or wood they'd cut and they'd get their sugar and tea and flour, just enough to last the winter. It seemed like a good way to live. It sounded like a good way to be happy. I guess that's why they call this the throwaway culture.

Deet read what he'd written. This kind of writing was so free, just say what you think. He looked through the book for another quotation.

Man is Nature's sole mistake.—W. S. GILBERT

That would make a good bumper sticker. Come to think of it, a lot of quotations would make good bumper stickers. Bumper stickers, the poor man's quotations. Wonder what Dan would make of this book.

Or:

The world is beautiful, but it has a disease called man.—FRIEDRICH NIETZSCHE

That was a good one. Pollution and killing all the animals off, and all that.

Deet's dad rattled out from under the Mercedes. It was almost closing time. Deet put his books and notebook back in his book bag and pulled on his parka.

Dad wiped his oily hands on a rag and then jerked his head at Deet.

"Come and look at this."

Deet had a pretty good idea what was coming. It was Wednesday, and that was the day the Snap-On tool guy came by with his truck to sell mechanics new tools. Dad couldn't resist them.

Deet looked at Bingo, who was still working in the next bay, sweat beaded on his fat face. Bingo winked at him, so Deet knew he was right.

Dad pulled open the top drawer of his toolbox and put the tools he'd been using back inside. The toolbox was as oily as everything else in the shop, and tools were piled higgledy-piggledy on the top of the chest. Deet wanted to wipe down every tool with gasoline and shine them up, clean out every drawer and line the bottoms with clean paper, line up all the tools in neat rows. He hated disorder and mess.

Taped on the open top lid of the box was a curling picture of Deet's mom, taken a few years back, when she was all dressed up.

When she got all dolled up, she looked so happy with herself. She'd do a little twirl on her high heels, earrings swinging. "How do I look?" His little sisters would be radiant with admiration, and Dad would look almost as tickled. But the way his mom dressed made Deet uncomfortable.

Dad pulled out a bottom drawer and took out a very big drive ratchet. "Three-quarter inch," he said. "Feel how heavy that is." Deet hefted the ratchet, watching Dad's face. It wasn't anything he'd want to drop on his foot, that was for sure.

"How much?" asked Deet.

"Seventy-five."

"Jeez."

"Don't tell Mom!" Dad looked about eight years old for a second, his long blond hair falling into his eyes. Deet couldn't help but smile at him.

They were both like that, his folks. They spend money on things they didn't need and sometimes didn't have enough left to buy what they did need. Whenever they got really broke, his folks would go out and buy something big. Like that red Corvette they'd had that didn't have enough room for all of them without squeezing up.

And it wasn't just money, it was planning and organization that got messed up. Things that needed doing on time, like getting the furnace cleaned, or the snow cleared off the roof. Warnings were never followed. Film was left in the glove compartment to fry, videocassettes were left on top of the television to de-magnetize, the kitchen filled with smoke because greasy spills were not immediately wiped off the bottom of the oven.

Deet could tell when something was going to go wrong, could tell when the money was going awry, when things had been done just too carelessly, when fixing was needed, or attention paid to details. He could tell, but there wasn't a thing he could do about it because he was only a kid.

Sometimes Deet felt like he was the only grown-up in the house.

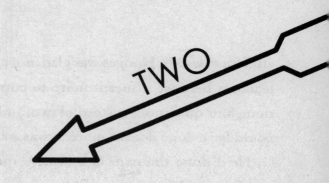

TWO

Deet was rereading the quota-

tion essays he'd written the night before for English class, eating his oatmeal kind of sideways so he wouldn't spill on his notebook, trying to imagine what Mr. Hodges would write about his comments.

The best thing about Mr. Hodges was that if you handed in your homework before first period, he'd have it corrected for you by English class at sixth period. And he didn't just write "good," or "needs more thought" at the top of the page. Mr. Hodges would write a lot, sometimes half a page. It was like having a great conversation with him.

The second best thing about Mr. Hodges was that he never made you talk in class if you didn't want to. Deet didn't like to talk in class.

And another good thing was that if you did extra

stuff for class Mr. Hodges was glad, not upset like some teachers because it meant more to correct. Deet had done four quotations instead of two, and he felt like he could have done dozens more, it was so much fun.

He'd done the man is a disease quotation and a good one by Mark Twain:

Good breeding consists of concealing how much we think of ourselves and how little we think of the other person.

(Out loud: Oh, Mrs. Jones, what a wonderful dress. To herself: My god, that woman's dresses are awful. I'm so glad *my* mother raised me to have taste.)

Jam and P. J. were having breakfast too, and the Formica tabletop was crowded with milk cartons and boxes of horrible cereal, Cocoa Puffs and Fruit Loops. Deet made himself oatmeal every morning, because he didn't approve of cold cereal.

Deet was into Good Food, and he despaired when his mother didn't seem to take such things seriously. She gave the girls potato chips for snacks and juice that wasn't 100 percent juice. Too much candy, too. He brought home printouts from his health class and made a few pointed comments, but that was all he could do. Both Mom and Dad were so agreeable, so uncritical, that it seemed wrong to find fault with them.

Once he'd complained to his mom about the *National Enquirer*s she bought at the supermarket. (Teenager gives birth to a chicken. Elvis's molecules found on Mars.)

"That stuff isn't true, you know," he'd said severely.

She had thrown a quick look at him, a small furrow between her eyes. "Well, they wouldn't print it if it wasn't true, would they?" She'd quit buying the *Enquirer,* though, and then Deet felt guilty that he'd spoiled something for her. It was like the time he'd tried to explain to her the difference between lie and lay, which she didn't use correctly. Now she hesitated and looked at him every time she used them. He didn't correct her English anymore.

P. J. was examining the cereal box in front of her through a haze of blond uncombed hair. "I can read this box!"

"Read it, then," said Jam.

"Fruit Loops," said P. J.

Jam opened her mouth to protest that that wasn't reading when Deet threw her a look. "That's good, Peej. You'll be reading the whole box at the end of the year," he said.

"*I* can read the whole box," said Jam.

"Well, I hope so. You're in the third grade."

Deet's mom scurried around the little kitchen in her pink bathrobe, her curls bobbing, packing the girls' lunches. Deet had made his the night before, as he always did. He never did things at the last minute if he could help it.

He took his bowl to the sink and rinsed it.

Jam suddenly put down her spoon and let out a wail.

"Mom, I forgot, I'm supposed to bring a picture for our family posters! A picture of our whole family!"

Mom stopped in her tracks and looked at Jam with consternation. "Today? Isn't that sort of short notice?"

"Well, she told us about it last week," Jam confessed, looking a little ashamed. Jam was inclined to be as disorganized as Mom and Dad.

"Oh, lord. Deet, will you please get out the box of pictures and find one for her?"

Deet made his world-weary face. "Come on."

He found the beat-up old shoe box full of snapshots on the bookshelf under a pile of Dad's car magazines and Mom's hairstyling magazines. He dumped the pictures out on the carpet and got on his knees to sort them out. Someone had spilled something red and sticky, like Kool-Aid, on the box lid, and some of the pictures were stuck together.

"Someday I have to put those in an album," his mom said as she passed through the living room. Deet smiled up at her, but he knew perfectly well that putting things in albums was not something his mom would ever do.

Jam and P. J. picked up this photo and that, squealing over pictures of themselves in diapers or with spaghetti smeared all over their faces.

Deet flipped through the pictures quickly, looking for the family picture they'd taken at Christmas, like they did every year. He and P. J. and Jam and Mom would all sit on the couch, and Dad would set the timer on the camera and then make a dash for the couch before the flash went off. In every picture Dad was a little blurred. Deet found the one he was looking for and gave it to Jam.

"Here. And take good care of it. I don't think we have another one. And next time, don't save your homework till the last minute."

Jam made a yah-yah face at him, and she and P. J. ran off to get dressed. Deet picked up the snapshots from the rug and stuffed them into the box. He had a while before the school bus came, so he got a wet paper towel and wiped the sticky stuff off the stuck-together photos. No serious damage.

He took the box into his room to sort.

Deet's room was in perfect order, his bedspread taut, his books organized logically, fiction on one shelf, nonfiction on the other. His thesaurus and dictionary lay on his desk, corners squared together, and neat lists were pinned precisely on the bulletin board, completed items crossed off with a ruled red line.

A map of the known universe was over his bed. Deet had had it laminated and had pinned a little sign on the solar system: You are here. Over the dresser was a history time line poster.

He could hear the rumpus from the girls' room as his mom got them ready for school.

"Patty Jane, you have to wear these pants today because the red ones are in the wash and it's too cold to wear a dress today."

"I hate these pants."

"Well, wear them anyway."

"Jam, go brush your teeth before you get that sweater on. You always get toothpaste splatters all over your clothes." P. J.'s belly laugh at this. "And P. J., put your inhaler in your pocket! Don't forget it today."

He turned on his cassette player to drown out their chatter. He'd been playing the same cassette for a week, because he was trying to learn by heart the words to "Alice's Restaurant," which he thought was very funny. He'd had to quit playing it in the living room, because P. J. started to learn it by heart as well, and he didn't think anyone would think "Alice's Restaurant" was suitable for a six-year-old. ("Mother stabbers! Father stabbers! Kill, kill, kill!")

Deet kept the volume low because Dad was still asleep. Dad had worked two jobs for a while now, trying to make a little extra, trying to catch up on the bills.

After he got off at the garage, he'd rush home to eat his dinner, then go to work driving a wrecker truck for an all-night wrecker service. He'd get home after midnight and be off to work again at eight the next morning. Deet was sure that he'd get tired with a killer schedule like that, but Dad seemed to have energy to burn. The bad thing was that the girls hardly got to see him except at dinner and on Sundays, when he didn't work, and except for dinner Deet saw him during the week only if he went to the garage after school.

Deet took some rubber bands from his desk drawer and started to make orderly piles of pictures on his bed. There was one picture of Mom with Deet when he was a baby. She was smiling joyfully at the camera, holding him on her hip. He was wearing only a diaper. He wondered who'd taken it. Deet turned it over to see if the date was on it. "Patty and Deet," she'd written. That was all. Patty was kind of a bubble-headed name, and she looked like a bubble-headed sort of girl in the picture. Nothing like a mother, that's for sure.

She'd come up north from the Midwest to get a job on the pipeline. She didn't have any folks. They'd been old when she was born and had died before she finished high school. Deet wished there was a picture of them, but his mom hadn't brought anything with her when she came north. Not even her memories, it seemed like, because she never talked about her life growing up. She got pregnant with Deet when she was just nineteen. She'd never told Deet who his father was, and he'd never asked. Not asking seemed like the courteous thing to do, and he wasn't very curious anyway.

It must have been pretty hard on her, all alone with a baby coming. But she told Deet she was happy to have him, because having a baby meant she had someone to love. He knew she wasn't just saying it to make him feel good, because he knew she was like that. All heart.

There was a blurry picture of the pipeline camp, taken from pretty far away. On the back she'd written "Dietrich," the name of the camp. That's where Deet got his name, though no one ever called him Dietrich.

There were two copies of Mom and Dad's wedding picture. They looked young, like kids, really. Mom looked like a model or something, with her stacked-up hairdo, and Dad was smiling so hard you could see the gap where his tooth was missing on the side.

Mom met Dad when Deet was still a baby, and he was a really nice guy. Deet had never seen him mad. He was tall and rangy with a sad kind of face. You look just like your dad, people told Deet, which was strange when they weren't even related, and because Deet had dark hair and dark eyes. Deet figured it was probably just that they used the same gestures, the kind of thing you pick up from living with someone. He picked up his last year's school picture and studied it. Maybe it was because he had kind of a sad face too.

There were a lot of good things about Charley Aafedt, but the thing Deet liked best about his dad was the way he could say something nice in a joking way. When someone pays you a compliment, it can be an awkward moment. You're not sure they really mean it, maybe it sounds a little phony or stiff. Dad wouldn't say seriously, "You did a good job cleaning the truck."

He'd make some joke like, "I'm going to get fat because Deet does all the work around here," and then they'd all laugh at the idea of Dad getting fat, but they'd know Deet was being praised.

Deet put all the pictures of Mom and Dad and himself in one pile and then he started on the pictures of the girls.

There were lots of Jam, because they'd had a new camera then. Mom had written "Jamima Mae Aafedt" on the back of every one, with the date, and how much she weighed at the time, "6 pounds ½ oz.," and exactly how old she was, like "3 months and 21 days." Like it was important, that half an ounce, three weeks instead of four. Proud mother.

Deet had been delighted when Jam was born, had hovered over her crib by the hour, letting her hold his finger in her tiny fist. There was a picture of him looking proud as punch, holding her in his lap. Jam's diaper was loose at the legs, and after the shutter had clicked she'd peed all over him.

Deet found the yellowish Polaroid picture the hospital had taken of P. J. when she was born. She looked wrinkled and crabby. Her tiny hospital bracelet was stapled to the corner. Patty Jane Aafedt. He riffled through the box, wondering if there was a bracelet for him or Jam as well, but there wasn't.

There were a lot fewer pictures of P. J. than there were of Jam. He hoped that wouldn't make P. J. feel bad.

Deet thought raising children was a very serious thing, and he wished his mom and dad were more systematic about it, and a little more careful about stuff like not taking enough pictures of the last baby. Or shots. When he read in the paper about the importance of inoculations and the shots needed for school, he asked his mom about P. J.'s and Jam's. She'd looked startled, that little line between her eyebrows.

"I know I have their shot records somewhere. I'll look for them and see if they're up-to-date." But of course she didn't do it until the last minute, after the school had sent out a couple of notices.

Dentist appointments and checkups, meetings with the teachers. Deet was always driving himself crazy trying to make sure his folks took care of those things.

Some jobs he'd just taken over for himself, like reading to the girls. He read to them every night, because he had heard that it was very important for their intellectual development.

Deet frowned at his stacks of photos and decided that he'd group them by years, not people. That would make more sense, and then you couldn't tell that P. J.'s stack was the smallest.

In a big manila envelope were more wedding pictures, snapshots. Deet in a little suit, squatting on the grass, eating a piece of cake from a plate at his feet. Grandma and Grandpa sitting stiffly at a table with balloons over it. It was hard to believe they'd even gone to the wedding, since Grandpa and Dad were not on good terms. Not that Dad ever said anything bad about Grandpa, but Grandpa had plenty to say about Dad. Deet thought Grandpa was the reason his Dad had that sad face.

Grandma and Grandpa had been a lot younger-looking in the wedding pictures. For sure that was the last time Grandpa'd ever been dressed up.

There were pictures of Bingo and Dan and Willy

all dressed up too. They looked completely wrong out of their overalls. Something about the wrists, the way they were holding their arms. How come some people could dress up and you didn't pay any attention, but with others, it was like they were wearing a Halloween costume or something?

Deet put all the pictures of old cars and trucks together and wrapped a rubber band around them. It was a big stack. Dad had taken pictures of all the cars and trucks he'd ever had, like they were people, both sides, front and back angles.

Deet put the sorted stacks of photos back in the box. Maybe he'd get an album this weekend and put them in it before someone spilled Kool-Aid on them again.

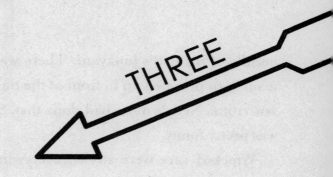

THREE

Deet was the first one to be

picked up on the west side run, so the bus was empty
when he got on, except for Mindy, the bus driver.

Mindy had been driving that route since Deet was
in kindergarten. She was a heavy, unpleasant woman
in her forties or so who had one of those jutting bull-
dog jaws and a down-turned mouth, but she always
grunted a greeting of sorts when he got on, more than
she did for the other kids. He always sat in the front seat,
behind her. It wasn't that he wanted her conversation,
he wanted to avoid the rest of the kids, who'd sprawl
over the seats and yell all the way to the school. Deet
jammed his fists in his pockets and burrowed his chin
into the collar of his parka. The bus hadn't warmed
up yet.

Nelly's stop was next. He lived in a trailer in the

middle of his dad's junkyard. There was a big home-made sign propped up in front of the trailer: NELSON'S BOUTIQUE. Nelly's mom had done that. She thought it was pretty funny.

Wrecked cars were strewn everywhere, behind a sagging fence, which was supposed to screen the cars from the road but didn't. Deet had been looking at that junkyard all his life, but he never saw it without a sort of mental shudder. If he'd had to live there he was sure he would have slit his own throat by now.

His own yard was bad enough. Dad had an old car in the back, a junker he was going to fix up and sell when he got around to it, and other stuff was scattered by the front porch: nylon-strap lawn chairs, wooden boxes, P. J.'s tricycle without a front wheel—almost buried in snow now, piles of lumber, and a stack of pallets, which Dad collected anywhere he could, on the theory that they'd be very useful someday.

When Deet went off to kindergarten, his mom used to ask him to bring kids home to play. Deet never wanted to bring anyone home from school, partly because there wasn't anybody in kindergarten he wanted to spend any more time with and partly because his house embarrassed him, even when he was in kindergarten. It didn't look anything like the houses in his Jan and Jerry reading books.

The house started out being an ordinary log cabin, which Dad had built the first summer he and Mom were married. That summer they'd all lived in the backyard in a tiny camper, one of those shells that fit on the back of a pickup, until the cabin was finished. The camper was still there, behind the house, in the willows.

After the girls were born, Dad had thrown up a frame addition on the side of the cabin that kind of spoiled the look of the cabin, and besides, he'd never gotten around to painting the addition. Deet was glad you couldn't see their house from the road where the bus stopped.

The bus stopped for Nelly, who was waiting by his driveway, on time for a change, shifting from foot to foot to stay warm. His arms were stiff at his sides, fists sucked up in his sleeves, just like a little kid. He threw himself down in the seat next to Deet, spikes of his hair standing on end in spite of the junk he'd smeared on it to make it lie down, his nylon GI surplus parka crackling from the cold. He threw a look of despair at Deet.

"Did you get your math done?"

"No."

"What do you mean, no?" Nelly squeaked. He was right in the middle of a voice change. "You always get your math finished."

"We're not having math today, remember? We're having that assembly. So I saved it until tonight."

Nelly rolled his eyes with relief. "Man, I forgot about that. Saved again."

Deet and Nelly had been in the same class since kindergarten, and Nelly always seemed to be hustling to keep up, treading water. It was because he wasn't organized, Deet thought. His notebooks were a scramble of papers, never clipped into the binder, falling out, and even his shirts weren't buttoned the right way, but started off on the wrong button.

Deet and Nelly were the only ones who lived off the main road. The rest of the kids who rode the bus lived in the fancy houses along the ridge, where everyone had a view of the valley and the mountains in the distance. Each house was better than the last one, and each yard was like a picture in a magazine. None of the kids who lived in those houses had their shirts buttoned wrong.

Deet's locker at school was right next to his homeroom. He usually put his stuff in his locker, took his homework to Mr. Hodges's room, and then took his library book to read until first period. He hoped no one would talk to him. He didn't like to talk. Small talk, people said. Making small talk. How are you? How's it going? What's up? There was nothing sensible to be said to those questions. Nonquestions.

His mom kept on urging him to make friends, but Dad said Deet was a loner, that's all there was to it. Deet didn't know if he was a loner or not. It was just that there were no other kids who were interested in the things he was interested in.

And he wasn't interested in what they were interested in. He just didn't get what sports were all about. Chasing a ball seemed silly enough, but even sillier was the way people took games so seriously.

Most of the new movies seemed to have car crashes or some idiotic guy, some action hero, and the new music bewildered him. He liked tunes you could hum, actually. He liked old stuff. Old movies, old music, like the big bands he heard on the radio once in a while. And books.

When he went to the library, there was no telling what he'd come home with. Last week he'd gotten a book on weaving, of all things, one on ancient armor, and two books by John Steinbeck, whom he'd just discovered in Mr. Hodges's class. (The book on weaving he got because he'd read in *National Geographic* that the Vikings had made their sails of wool, and the threads that went one way were made with the undercoat of a special sheep and the threads that went the other way were made with the top coat. So he wondered what other interesting things there might be to learn about weaving.)

The thing about books was that someone, somewhere, had written them, and so people somewhere must be reading them. Even the ones he took from the library had due dates stamped in the back, which showed that someone in town was reading them. So why did he never meet anyone who read things like that, or talked about them, or wrote them? And why didn't anyone ever talk the way they did in books?

Deet was just different, that's all. He'd always been different from everyone he knew, and he guessed he always would be. The thing was not to let people know how different he was if he could help it. The best way to do that was to keep his mouth shut.

Deet was frowning over his book when Nelly took the seat next to him in the back row of homeroom. Nelly tipped his chair back on its back legs so it leaned against the wall, clasped his hands behind his head, and watched while the front rows filled up with their classmates. Nelly didn't hang out with anyone any more than Deet did, but he was always very interested in what everyone else did and pointed out this and that to Deet, who never paid any attention.

Nelly suddenly tipped his chair forward to rest on four legs and looked urgently at Deet.

"Would you take the second bus and help me with those equations? I just can't get it, no matter what."

Deet started to nod an okay, but then he remembered.

"Jeez, I'm sorry, Nelly, but I got to go over to my Grandpa's right after school."

Nelly mimed desperation, banging his head on his desk. Deet had to laugh.

"Why don't you call me tonight, Nell, and I'll talk you through it, okay?" Nelly looked dubious about the efficiency of this method, but he agreed.

Deet had been helping Nelly for years, and not just Nelly. Teachers often asked Deet to help someone out, someone who'd been absent, or someone who was floundering. He supposed it was because his notes were always neat and complete, because he didn't think he was any good at explaining stuff. He didn't think he had the patience to teach anybody anything.

Sometimes it seemed to Deet that he was surrounded by people who couldn't organize or plan, and sooner or later they always managed to catch him up in their mess.

At sixth period Mr. Hodges handed back their quotations notebooks. He'd written comments on all of Deet's pages, and at the bottom of the last one he'd written: "Your writing shows logical and coherent thought, which gives me hope for the future of humanity!" Deet pinched his lips together so that his face wouldn't show how pleased he was.

On the bus ride to Grandpa's house he tilted his book toward the streetlights so he could mark all the quotations he wanted to write about for the next week's homework. He found one he liked right away.

At fifty everyone has the face he deserves.
—GEORGE ORWELL

Did Grandpa and Grandma have the faces they deserved? What other kinds of faces could they have? Grandma's face was soft and doughy. It just didn't have anything in it at all. Maybe that's how Grandma was. Not up to much. Grandpa was the opposite. His face was rock hard, and there weren't many wrinkles, no smile lines around his eyes or mouth because he didn't smile, or even frown.

Deet was very careful at his grandfather's house, trying to avoid Grandpa's sarcasm ("Born in a barn?") when you didn't shut the door fast enough, or Grandma's picky complaints ("Don't sit in that chair with those dirty pants!").

He swept the snow off his feet outside the front door, stepped inside the porch and removed his boots, set them neatly in the corner, and knocked on the door. Here everything was organized and precisely planned the way he always wanted things to be at home, but there was something wrong with it. There was something cold and gray about organization at his grandparents' house.

His grandmother came to the door, looking fake surprised—"Look who's here, Grandpa!"—though she certainly knew he was coming because she'd called his mom to ask that he be sent over after school.

She was thick and stocky, with short gray hair like all the grandmas in the world seemed to have. He'd seen pictures of her when she was young, and she didn't look anything like she did now. Maybe getting fat erased all your own features and made you look like everyone else. Grandpa didn't have a bit of fat on him, so he looked a lot the way he did in his old pictures. But Grandma had lost all her distinguishing features. They'd been blurred and erased, and now she was a sort of generic grandma.

She sat back down at the kitchen table where her sewing basket was and picked up the pair of Grandpa's black work pants she'd been patching.

"How was school today, Deet?" she asked as she always did.

"Fine, Grandma," he answered as he always did.

Inside the house everything was neat and clean and quiet. They never had the radio on, and Grandpa wouldn't allow a television in the house. Hard to imagine Dad as a little boy in this silent house. Maybe people become the way they are because they want to be the opposite of their parents, like he wanted to be all organized and efficient. Maybe Dad had wanted to be happy-go-lucky instead of being wrapped too tight like Grandma and Grandpa.

Their house had its own smell, which Deet could never identify. Dad said it was sourdough in a crock on top of the cabinets, which Grandma used nearly every morning for hotcakes. Maybe it was, but there was something else that smelled like meanness.

Maybe it was the smell of dead animals. The bearskin nailed against the living room wall, moose horns nailed over the porch door.

There were three guns hanging on the wall, a .22, a .30-06, and a .357. Grandpa'd go hunting every fall for a moose, and shoot forty or fifty spruce hens as well, which Grandma plucked and put in the freezer. He prided himself on providing the meat.

That was one of the big problems between Grandpa and Dad. Dad wouldn't hunt. He hated killing things. When he turned eighteen he left the mining camp and went to mechanic school. And he wouldn't go hunting with his father anymore. Dad let Deet make up his own mind about hunting, but Deet had shaken his head no when Grandpa wanted to take him out for spruce hens the first time. He didn't want to kill things either. "You're making an old woman out of this boy," Grandpa snarled at Dad, "just like you."

The stove gleamed and a shining teakettle sat in its

place on the back burner. On the wall by the stove was a framed picture of hands, just hands, no face, no arms, just hands, praying. Deet had always disliked that picture. It gave him the creeps.

What was the point of praying, anyway? If this god was all-powerful, all-knowing, he knew about someone's troubles already, didn't he? Once Deet had asked Grandpa about this. Grandpa's eyes had snapped blue sparks. "You know," he said, "you can go to hell for asking questions like that just as sure as you can from stealing." Well, if he was a good god, he wouldn't have to be asked to do a good thing for someone, would he? He'd just *do* it. Mom said the good thing about Deet was that he'd do stuff without being asked. She said it was twice as good to have a favor if you didn't have to ask for it. Shouldn't this god be like that? Should he have to be begged?

Like those prayer things organized for someone in the hospital. "We all prayed for you to get well." Like god kept a tally. *Okay. Three hundred and seventy-five prayers. I guess I can heal him now.* Or what about, *Only two hundred prayers. Not enough. Let him die.*

Deet didn't believe in god at all, because everything people said about god was so silly. Illogical. Another way he was different from everyone he knew.

The curtains hung stiffly at the window, and the braided rug sat where it always sat, precisely in front of the rocker.

His grandfather sat in the rocker as he usually sat, and he gave Deet a critical look before he folded the newspaper and stood up. The look, Deet was sure, indicated that he thought Deet should have been there earlier.

"I just got off the bus," he said in answer to that look. His grandfather grunted.

Even though he wasn't really Deet's grandfather, he never seemed to make any distinction between Deet and the girls. He always treated Deet the same as the girls, but it was not as if there was a lot of enthusiasm over any of them.

Grandma kept pictures on the bookcase in the dark living room: Dad at eight or nine, looking no different from his grown-up self; pictures of the girls as babies; a picture of Mom and Dad and Deet before the girls were born. There was a picture from the mine, the year they had such a big clean-up, Grandpa posing proudly with the gold pan full of nuggets and gold dust.

Grandpa's parents had brought him from Finland when he was just a baby. Deet had read that the Finns had been invaded by hordes from Mongolia, and that was why some Finns had slanted eyes and broad cheekbones. Grandpa certainly would have approved of Genghis Khan, who was not an old woman.

"Have something to eat first, if you want, and then I want you to help me with the propane bottles." Those bottles were hundred pounders, and Grandpa had handled them all by himself for as long as Deet had been around. Now he was asking Deet for help. Deet looked quickly into Grandpa's face, but it was stony, no answers there.

"I'm not hungry," said Deet. He put his boots back on and went out with Grandpa to carry the five bottles into the woodshed.

FOUR

The night it happened was a

cold, hard night, thirty below. Ice fog covered everything, but by the light from the kitchen window Deet could see frost crusted on the trees by the house, bowing the branches with its weight.

He was doing his homework at the kitchen table. He usually did his homework in his room, but when the weather turned cold Deet's room was the coldest in the house, because the heat registers weren't working right. Dad was going to get around to fixing it this weekend, he said.

Deet was having a hard time concentrating on his social studies book, the Constitution this week, because his mom was washing the dishes and chattering away as she usually did while she worked. She was telling him, word for word, the plot of the movie she'd seen last night on television. Some World War II thing about a guy in a German prison camp. Actually, it sounded interesting, and Deet had to frown hard at the Bill of Rights to stay in focus. The television in the living room was on too loud as usual.

P. J. and Jam were already in their pajamas, playing on the living room carpet, surrounded by their Barbie dolls, which Deet hated, because Barbies never seemed to have anything on their little minds but clothes and Ken. He was irritated by the tone of voice they used when they played with Barbies, the tone that implied that whatever was happening in Barbie's little world, it was of great importance, the center of the universe, in fact, the highest development of civilization. When he was finished outlining the Bill of Rights he was going to sabotage their little plastic lives, give them something real to worry about, like nuclear disaster, or cancer, or something.

Deet had just discovered that his social studies book was sitting in a little puddle of ketchup left over from dinner, and he was trying to wipe it off with a paper towel when the phone rang.

His mom dashed to the phone, a dish towel thrown

over her shoulder and a pot in her hand, breathless when she answered. It was her long, long silence after she said hello that made Deet look up from his book. She seemed to freeze on the spot, and she didn't say a thing, except "Yes." Then she hung up, her face absolutely still.

The television announcer's silly, enthusiastic voice blared in the living room.

"Put the girls to bed, Deet," she said. She didn't look at him.

Deet lowered his eyes to the table. The blood felt as if it were draining from his face, leaving his skin feeling tight and itchy. He could hear his heart begin to thump hard, could hear his blood pounding in his ears.

Something terrible had happened, just as he'd always thought it would.

A dozen things might have happened. An accident. Maybe Dad had had an accident. Maybe Grandpa had had a heart attack. No, none of those things. She would have said something like, "Where is he? I'll be right there." She hadn't said a thing. This was something worse, something there were no words for.

When he got up from the table, his knees were shaky. He went into the living room to get the girls.

"Pick up your stuff. Mom wants you to go to bed." His voice was as shaky as his knees. P. J. started to collect the fluffy little bits of Barbie clothes, minuscule shoes, tiny purses, but Jam charged into the kitchen. "Mom, just a little while longer?"

Deet went back to the kitchen to collect Jam, and he could see that she had seen their mom's face.

Deet put his hand in the middle of Jam's back and propelled her toward the door. Jam gave another glance at their mother before she left the kitchen. Before Deet could follow her, P. J. dashed into the kitchen and searched for her favorite cup in the dish rack, the pink plastic one with the ballerina.

"Mom, there's this boy at school who has a baby fox," she said. She'd turned on the faucet and was testing the running water with her fingers, waiting until it was just cold enough. "I wish we had a fox. That would be really cool." She filled her glass and drank it down, then turned to see if there was even the smallest hope of getting a fox and saw her mother's face. P. J. looked quickly at Deet, who jerked his head at her to tell her to come. She put the glass down and followed Deet.

As soon as they were in their bedroom, P. J. asked, "Is Mom mad at us?"

"No, silly," said Deet. He couldn't think of anything to head them off, so he said, "She's just worried about something." Both girls blinked at him, stony faced. He was sorry he'd said that, because Mom never worried about anything, so it certainly wasn't going to reassure them that everything was all right. So he said sternly, "Get into bed by the time I count three or I won't read anything!"

Jam jumped into her bed with mock-fearful screams. P. J. arranged her bears in the certain way she said they liked to sleep, while Jam contorted her pillow into the right shape. Deet pulled the book of fairy tales from the shelf by the door. It didn't have any illustrations, so he could sit in the corner by the window and read until they fell asleep, and they wouldn't be continually asking to look at the pictures.

He started with the first one in the book, about the twelve dancing princesses, who always reminded him of Barbie dolls themselves, thinking of nothing but parties and dances. Ordinarily he would read the story with sarcastic asides, but tonight he read woodenly, not knowing a word he read. Jam fell asleep halfway through, but P. J. was still awake, so he read the one about the Pied Piper. It took another fifteen minutes before P. J. fell asleep. He wished he could read forever and never stop. As soon as he stopped he was going to have to know what was happening to them.

By the time he'd finished reading, his knees had stopped feeling so shaky and a hard, dead feeling had taken over his stomach. He closed the book and looked at their clean little faces and felt a stab of sorrow that he couldn't protect them from whatever dreadful thing was coming.

He shut the door to the girls' room and went to look for his mother. She wasn't in the kitchen. He found her sitting on the edge of her bed, holding her stomach and rocking back and forth. The pot was on the floor by her feet, and she had the dish towel wadded against her mouth.

"What was that call about? What's wrong?"

She didn't look at him, just kept rocking. Mom, who never stopped talking, unable to speak. He put his hand on her shoulder and shook her, his voice husky with panic. "Mom, tell me. Is Dad hurt?"

She took a deep shuddering breath and looked at him at last. Then she began to cry silently, the way Jam did when she scraped her knee or something, her mouth square. And just like Jam, when she stopped crying she could hardly speak for the hiccupy gasps, so Deet wasn't sure he heard her right.

"He's been arrested! He's in jail!"

"Jail," said Deet, as if he'd never heard of it.

She dropped the dish towel and doubled over again.

"They caught him with drugs on the way to work. They pulled him over for a headlight, and they found drugs." She rocked in anguish, her head nearly touching her knees.

The headlight. Who would drive in ice fog, in the dark long winter nights, with one headlight out? Dad would. Deet had worried about it. "I'll get to it tomorrow," Dad had said. A surge of fury made Deet's head throb. Stupid. *Stupid*.

Then it hit him what she'd said. Drugs? Dad? That couldn't be right. There was no way his dad would have anything to do with drugs. He didn't even drink, just a beer every once in a while.

"It's a mistake, Mom," Deet told her. "Dad wouldn't do drugs. That's crazy."

She looked at him. "It's not a mistake."

She covered her face with her hands and began to cry again.

All those classes they'd had in school about drugs. He'd never even gotten the names straight. It had seemed to have nothing to do with him. How you could tell if someone was using drugs. The eyes. Change in disposition. Some other stuff he'd forgotten. Dad was not some drugged-out idiot like they were talking about.

They sat on the edge of her bed for a long time, silent. Deet thought he should get up, make her some coffee, but when he stood up, she grabbed his hand.

"He wanted to keep that wrecker job. So Gary, the new tire guy, gave him something that would keep him awake, give him energy." She stared furiously at the wall. "Gary," she said with loathing, as if she could see him there.

"I thought it was a terrible idea, and I told him just to quit, we'd get by without his working two jobs. He said it wouldn't do any harm, but it did, Deet. He was so jittery, and he couldn't sleep, even after he'd put in sixteen hours at work."

Deet sat down on the bed again and tried to think.

Deet had a terrible thought. "Grandpa," he said.

They stared at each other, wide-eyed.

"Does he have to know?" Deet asked.

She squeezed her eyes shut tight. "Everyone will have to know, Deet."

The newspaper. Marriage licenses, divorces, and births.

Police blotter, list of arrests, court column.

Everybody read those. Tomorrow maybe, Dad would be in the newpaper, and everyone would know. All the kids at school. Mr. Hodges. Mr. *Hodges*. What about P. J. and Jam? When they went to school, some horrible kids would say, *Your dad's in ja-il, your dad's in ja-il.* Dan and Willy and Bingo. With the cold weather they were working double time, and how would they make out without Dad?

Deet was sick with shame. It hadn't done any good to not talk in class, to sit in the back row, to stay away from people. He was going to be stared at anyway, he was going to be exposed. Deet wished he never had to leave the house, never had to see a human being again, he felt so ashamed.

What if there were some way to turn time backward. What if you had one chance to push a button and then that day had never happened, you could start all over again on the day before, only you could make sure that whatever it was wouldn't happen again. If only you had one more chance before the world came to an end. If only you could do that one thing that would keep the disaster from happening.

When Deet finally went to bed, he stared at the ceiling and began to think about all the jail movies he'd seen. Nightmares of cold cement, bars and beatings, fights, attacks, indescribable terrors. The cold clang of the cell doors. Those fat, sullen guards. Dad in there with horrible criminals, murderers. Gentle, cheerful Dad. Deet wanted to put his arms around him, to protect him from this thing that had happened to him.

It wasn't the first time he'd felt helpless being just a kid, but it was the worst.

FIVE

When Deet woke up the next

morning, for a minute he didn't remember what had happened, but he felt something dark and horrible hanging around the bed. Then he remembered.

Dad was in jail.

He got up and was sick in the bathroom. The acid from his stomach burned his throat. He brushed his teeth and rinsed his mouth to get rid of the taste. Then he sat on the edge of the bathtub and looked at the faded pink towels draped carelessly on the rack. Mom's hair dryer, hair spray, face creams, the toothpaste cap on the floor. Everything looked dangerous and unreal.

While he pulled on his clothes, he could hear his mom talking on the telephone, her voice low and tight. She didn't sound like herself. Deet never thought about going to school that day, never thought about waking the girls up. Their regular life had ended, it seemed, as thoroughly as if they'd been kidnapped by aliens and dropped on the moon.

When he heard the back door shut, Deet walked stiffly to the kitchen. It smelled like fresh coffee, the way it usually smelled. He ached all over, as if he had the flu. He heard the car start. It was very cold out still, and if Mom were going out she'd have to let it run for a while to heat up.

When she came back in, Deet asked, "Where are you going?"

"I made an appointment to talk to a lawyer." She was very pale, and she wore no earrings or makeup; her hair was pulled back and fastened at her neck. She looked older. Deet wondered how she could move, make herself start the car, get things done. He felt drained and limp, as if everything would be too much effort.

"How'd you know what lawyer to call?"

"Yellow Pages," she said.

She was different today. Hard to believe she'd seemed helpless with crying last night. Now she looked like someone else, someone hard and purposeful. Deet didn't know how that had happened. She began to put on her winter gear, snow pants and heavy boots, and then she poured herself a cup of coffee. She sat on the edge of her chair to drink it, everything about her urgent.

"Dad said I can see him today. I'll call to find out when. You watch the girls and try to keep their minds off this, will you, Deet? Play Chutes and Ladders with them or something."

When she zipped her parka up, Deet could see that her hands were shaking. Before she went out, she turned to him.

"Maybe you should find a way to tell them, Deet. They'll know something's wrong when they wake up and Dad and I are both gone. You always know how to talk to them."

He waited until Mom's car had pulled out of the driveway, and then he went outside to get the newspaper.

Deet had been thinking about the newspaper since he woke up. He was ashamed to be worrying so much about people knowing what had happened to Dad. He was ashamed that he'd thought first of what this meant to him, Deet, not what it meant to Dad, or Mom or the girls. He was pretty sure it didn't speak very well for his character.

That ordinary newspaper sticking out of the delivery box looked evil, horrible. He took it inside and smoothed it out on the kitchen table, his stomach in a twist. Waves of cold came off the paper as he smoothed it, and the smell of ink. This newspaper, an everyday thing, had turned into something dangerous, terrifying.

Deet turned to the page that listed arrests and scanned it fast, looking for Dad's name. Nothing about Dad. Too soon, of course. The arrests listed had taken place a few days before.

Deet let himself breathe again. Maybe it wouldn't *ever* be in the paper. Maybe no one would know. Maybe they'd just let Dad go. Maybe it wasn't any big deal.

He began to read the listings again, more carefully. There was one guy arrested, stopped for speeding. Found illegal substances. Taken to the correctional facility. Deet felt his face go white again, and he felt weak. That was no different from Dad. If that guy was in the paper, Dad would be too.

He'd never known before that the stories in the newspaper were nothing but words, told nothing real, left out all the stuff that made you know what it had been like for the people in the stories.

What did that man arrested for drugs say when they stopped him? Was he scared? Did they handcuff him? Did they make him spread out against the car while they searched him, like in the movies? Did he call his family to tell them he was in jail? Were his family waiting at home now, like Deet and the girls, waiting for more terrible things to happen?

Deet read the arrest column over again slowly a third time, and he began to worry about the things he hadn't thought of last night. What if Dad had to stay in jail for a long time? Could he keep his job? Would Dan let him work on cars? Deet imagined an unpleasant-looking customer saying, "I don't want Charley Aafedt working on my car. He's probably all doped up!" Dad wouldn't be earning any money locked up in jail. Money was why this had happened, and now it was going to be worse.

What about the medical insurance? What if P. J. had an asthma attack, how would they pay for that? Where was Dad's truck? It wasn't much good, but with the winter so cold they needed two vehicles in case one wouldn't start or something. It was always happening when it was fifty below. Maybe they wouldn't give it back to him.

He read the arrest column one more time, and words he'd never paid attention to before leaped out at him, stunned him with their power to hurt. Officer so-and-so, incarcerated, correctional center, illegal substance.

Deet went into his bedroom and sat at his desk. He pulled a pad of paper and a pencil toward him. He started to write down all the jail words he could think of, pressing hard with the pencil.

incarceration
imprisonment
captive, captured, caught
accused
convicted

criminal
crook
inmate
offender
Department of Corrections

Corrections? Like erasing a mistake and writing the right word in? Or like someone corrects your speech and then you say it right. Correctly. Somebody does something wrong and the law will correct him. You go to jail and you're corrected. Now you have it right, they say, patting you on the head when they let you out. "Corrections" was a stupid word for jail.

rehabilitation
felon
convicted, a convict, a con
misdemeanor

Your demeanor is not right, it's a mistake, it needs correction.

He couldn't think of any more, so he looked up

words for "jail" in the thesaurus. There were dozens of them.

The slammer. That must be because of the iron doors, the noise they made when they shut, the sound bouncing off the cement-block walls, like in the movies. *Cell.* Like bees, like monks, small and tight. *Stir, stir-crazy, hoosegow,* like in the old country songs. *Lockup. The pen, penitentiary.* Where people are penitent? Sorry for their crimes? *Hard time, chain gang.*

"Alice's Restaurant." He'd thought it was funny, the part when Arlo went to jail.

Deet sat back and stared at the list.

All over the world, since the beginning of history, there had been jails and prisons and dungeons, and people had been captured and locked up. A million billion people had had this done to them. Why had he never thought about it? Now that he had, he felt that he'd been surrounded by these words all his life, but they were invisible. Some things were invisible until they happened to you.

The radio, TV, songs. "Birmingham jail, love, Birmingham jail. Send me a letter to the Birmingham jail." Go directly to jail, do not pass go, do not collect $200.

He used to say jail, like everybody else. A joke, a casual word. Nothing to do with him. Now that word seemed sharp and hard and full of pain.

SIX

After he'd finished his list, he

lay back on his bed. He pulled the covers over his head and curled into a tight ball. He wished he could live the rest of his life in a cave, completely hidden. He fell asleep for a little while, and though he couldn't remember what he had been dreaming, he knew it was awful. P. J. and Jam woke him up, tugging at his shirt. He blinked at them.

"Deet, where're Mommy and Daddy? Aren't we going to school today?" P. J. asked. Jam must have seen something in his face, because she suddenly looked terrified.

"Did someone die? Is it *Daddy*?" she whispered.

Deet laughed a phony sort of laugh, but before it was finished he'd thought that maybe going to jail was a lot like dying. Maybe even worse, because there was no blame in dying. No shame.

"God, you're silly, Jam. Of course not. I'm going to make us breakfast now, and you guys get dressed. And then we'll play Chutes and Ladders."

There was no response, though usually playing Chutes and Ladders was their idea of heaven.

"I'll make pancakes," he said. There wasn't anything they liked better, so that ought to be worth something.

But they were still looking hard at Deet. They'd been happy little girls all their lives, not a worry in the world. They didn't even know that there were troubles in the world. Everything had been wonderful for them, they didn't know anything. And now here was this look on their faces, and he had to tell them something.

Deet cleared his throat and sat up.

"It's like this. Dad did something wrong, against the law, and so he can't come home until it's all taken care of."

"Is Dad a robber?" asked P. J.

"Jeez, P.J!" Deet exploded. "No! You know Dad wouldn't do something like that!"

Deet thought that he would have said that about drugs as well, but it made him feel almost better for a second. No matter what, Dad didn't do anything to hurt anyone else. He'd hurt himself, but he didn't rob anyone. Or kill anyone.

They were still waiting, so he swung his feet over the side of the bed and put his elbows on his knees and looked into their faces.

"You remember when Dad was talking about his headlight, and he said it didn't work and he had to get it fixed?"

They both nodded.

"Well, he didn't get it fixed, and the cops stopped him last night. It's against the law to drive with just one light." *Oh god,* Deet thought. *Now I've done it. I've lied to them. They're going to find out, for sure. They're not so dumb that they'll buy this for long. They'll know you can't go to jail for something like this.*

"Silly Daddy," said P. J. with a frown. She was trying to sound grown-up, Deet knew.

Jam was watching Deet carefully. "When is he coming home? Will the police hurt Daddy? Will they take his truck away? Is Daddy sad?"

Jam could think up a lot of questions fast.

P. J. made a face. "Grandpa is going to be really mad at Dad."

Deet shot a quick look at P. J. He hadn't known that the girls had picked up on the problems between Dad and Grandpa.

"Yeah," said Deet. "He'll be mad all right. But we're not mad. Anybody can make a mistake, right? Remember the time I broke the car window with that two-by-four, and remember the time you girls ran the bathwater so high it spilled all over the floor and Dad had to take the floorboards out to fix it? Anybody can make a mistake."

Jam nodded. "Even Grandpa can make a mistake," she said. They were all quiet a minute, trying to think of a mistake Grandpa had made, but they couldn't.

They heard the car pull into the driveway, the crunch of tires on packed snow. The girls looked at Deet and he felt sick again. In a few minutes they'd hear things they didn't want to know.

Mom slammed the back door, which was hard to shut because of the frost buildup. Deet needed to scrape the frost away with a kitchen knife again.

She hung her purse up on the hook behind the door and bent down to take her boots off. Deet couldn't see her face.

"Did you kids eat breakfast?" she asked, and Deet could tell she was trying to talk in her normal voice. With her back to them she unzipped her parka and hung it up. She was doing these things more slowly, more deliberately, than she usually did. *Trying to get control,* Deet thought.

"We just got up," he said. "I'm going to make us some hotcakes." Deet wished he hadn't mentioned hotcakes. He felt heavy with grief, and everything seemed like too much work.

"Go get dressed, girls," Mom said.

"Mommy," P. J. began.

"Get dressed," Mom said firmly. "I want to talk to Deet for a minute."

When the girls left, she pulled off her snow pants and then sat heavily in a kitchen chair and began to talk fast.

"There are a lot of steps to go through. It's very complicated, and I don't understand any of it. First of all is the arraignment, when they decide what to do with Dad, and then there are hearings and all sorts of things." Her voice took on a higher pitch. "Then a trial. A *trial*. It's not real, it's like a TV show." Deet was afraid she was going to lose control again. "What did you say to the girls?" she asked.

"That Dad got busted for a broken headlight."

She gave him an unsatisfied look, and he could tell she was as unhappy as he was to let them think a lie.

"I called Dan to tell him what happened. It was Gary who answered the phone. That creep."

Deet threw an anxious look at her. He'd never heard her say a mean word about anyone before. She got up to hang up her snow pants, then looked down at her stocking feet and started searching for her shoes among the heap of shoes and slippers by the door. She turned to him suddenly. "I called Grandpa this morning. It was horrible. He started to yell and said they'd have nothing to do with Dad. He said terrible things about him." Mom began unwrapping the scarf from around her neck, but she stopped as her face suddenly crumpled. "My poor Charley," she said.

Deet found her shoes and handed them to her.

"When can you see Dad?"

"At two. I'm going at two."

"Can I come with you?"

Mom gave him a horrified look. "Of *course* not. What are you thinking? The jail is a terrible place, full of terrible people. I can hardly stand to go myself."

Deet felt immediate relief. "You shouldn't go alone," he said. *What a phony,* he thought. He didn't want to go. He didn't want to ever leave the house, much less go to a jail, a prison.

She gave him a sad smile, just a sort of tuck in the corners of her mouth, and bent to put her shoes on.

They were at the table eating pancakes, or pretending to eat pancakes, when there was a knock on the back door. Deet and his mother jumped as if they'd never heard a knock at the door before. They looked at each other, wide-eyed with dread. The police? The newspapers? Grandpa? God, don't let it be Grandpa.

Mom wrenched the door open and Sally Chambers from down the street came in with a swirl of icy fog.

She took the empty chair and pulled her coat off. P. J. leaned toward her and said in a whisper, "Dad's in jail."

"I heard about Charley," Sally told Mom.

Mom blinked back tears and looked down at the table. "How?"

"You know, Bingo's a friend of Sam's."

Deet scraped his chair back and got up to leave. Sally frowned at him. "Look at me, Deet. You think this is the end of the world, but it isn't. I spent some time in that jail when I was eighteen. Same reason, too."

"You didn't get your headlight fixed either, Sally?" asked Jam.

Deet's mom looked at Sally, puzzled. "I didn't know that."

"Well, I guess it just never came up." Sally said. "I'm not proud of being so stupid, but I'm not really ashamed of it either. People make mistakes. That's all there is to it."

"That's just what Deet said," Jam said thoughtfully.

Deet sat back down and stared at Sally for a minute. How could someone spend time in a nightmare place like jail and it didn't show?

After Sally left, Deet went to his room to try to do some homework. He had some biology drawings to do, but he couldn't even make himself pick up the pencil.

Then he looked up "prison" in the quotation book. There was nothing there, or under "jail," so he looked under "crime." There were only two quotations.

Poverty is the mother of crime.
—MARCUS AURELIUS

If poverty is the mother of crimes, want of sense is the father of them.—JEAN DE LA BRUYERE

Deet sadly read the last one again. That one certainly had it right. He looked under "trouble."

I have certainly known more men destroyed by the desire to have a wife and child and keep them in comfort than I have seen destroyed by drink and harlots.
—WILLIAM BUTLER YEATS

Well, he could sure see that. He wrote that quotation in his notebook, and he chewed on his pencil for a while before he wrote why he liked the quote.

It's really hard to earn a living and try to keep everybody happy. Spend enough time with everyone, buy all those Barbie clothes. Maybe if you're the breadwinner you feel guilty all the time when you think of the things you can't buy for your family. Maybe you feel really jealous when you see those fancy houses, or those big Dodge trucks pulling a trailer with two snowmobiles on it.

SEVEN

After Sally left, Mom got ready

to go to the jail. Everything depended on Dad. Only after she'd seen him would they know how he was, how they would be able to stand this thing.

But Deet couldn't imagine what Dad would be like. He tried to imagine Dad in some other totally extraordinary place: He tried Dad backstage, putting on makeup for a Broadway musical. Or standing up in front of a crowd of people, asking them to vote for him. But Dad in jail just couldn't be imagined.

The lawyer had explained that Mom mustn't be late. The jail was very strict about visiting hours, and you would not be allowed in if you were so much as a minute late. Being on time was not one of Mom's best skills, and it was her experience that no matter how much you wanted to be on time, something would happen to make you late. The car wouldn't start, or Jam would throw up, or the toilet would overflow, or the clock would stop. So Deet fretted, watching the clock, and Mom dressed carefully, an hour before she had to leave, warmed up the car long before it was necessary, and left with time to spare.

Before she left, Deet finally got the girls involved in a game of Chutes and Ladders, though it was all he could do to sit through it, he was so jumpy. The girls had relaxed, and maybe he had too. A bit.

Deet thought what Sally said had made a difference, had made it all seem more normal. If you take some horrible thing and divide it among a lot of people, it wasn't as horrible anymore. He wondered if there was a quotation about that.

Deet fidgeted the whole time his mom was gone, giving the girls offhand, automatic answers, feeling more like a recording or a robot than a real person. He kept trying not to look nervous to the girls, and that seemed to make him act weirder than ever, his gestures all wrong, his voice up there in some phony-cheery range.

After they heard Mom's car pull into the driveway, it seemed to take her forever to come up the front steps and open the door. Deet scanned Mom's face to see what was there. Nothing. She seemed to have discovered in just one day how to mask her feelings, pretend.

She chattered brightly to the girls as she hung up her clothes on the hooks by the door. "Daddy is fine and sends you his love. He can call you on the phone pretty soon, when he gets his phone privileges."

"But when can he come *home*," asked Jam in a whiny kind of way.

"Well, we don't know for sure, but it will be a while."

"Will he be here for Easter?"

"I just don't know yet."

When the girls had wandered off to watch TV, Mom poured herself a cup of coffee. She made a face because the coffee was left over from breakfast, had been sitting there all day getting stronger and stronger. Deet wished he'd thought to make her a fresh pot. He seemed to be having a hard time thinking about other people today. He was concentrating too hard on keeping himself together. He seemed on the edge of tears all the time.

Some scrap of music from the radio, something that reminded him of Dad, a magazine cover, a look on Mom's face would set him off. Deet could see that she had lost some of that hard efficiency she'd started out with in the morning, and when she was alone with him, she looked as close to tears as he felt.

"It was horrible," she said, staring into the murky coffee in the cup. An ugly place, full of guards, and there was this terrible woman at the desk who'd looked at her in a certain way when she signed in. She'd had to say Dad's name out loud when the guard asked who she was visiting, and she couldn't. She'd whispered it, ashamed for everyone to hear his name. And Dad, Dad had looked awful.

"He's in a prison uniform, Deet. Just like everybody else there."

Deet had a vision of Dad in a striped suit, like the comic books, but the picture was so impossible that it melted away as soon as it had come.

"I told him what the lawyer said, that he'd be in to visit him in a day or two to let him know what was going on. Dad's worried about you."

"Me?"

"He thinks you'll have a hard time of it at school."

Deet, of course, was worried about that too, so he couldn't think of anything to say.

"And he thinks you'll be ashamed of him," Deet's mom said.

The tears jumped into his eyes. He *had* felt ashamed. It was true. He stared at the table and bit his lip until the pain made him forget about crying. He still couldn't look at her, but he said, "I'll never be ashamed of him."

EIGHT

On Monday, Dad's arrest was

in the police column.

Deet had imagined seeing it there so many times that he'd taken the edge off of it, but it still made him sick to actually see Dad's name there, to read the cold details. Drugs. It sounded so sleazy, so sordid.

He could imagine everyone in the town reading it. Grandma and Grandpa. The guys at work. Parents, asking their kids, "Don't you have a boy in your class named Aafedt?"

The day after that, Deet went back to school. He didn't take the bus. He asked Mom to drive him because he didn't think he could stand to feel the eyes on the back of his neck.

They'd once had a hermit crab that changed its shell for a bigger one when it grew out of the old one.

Deet and the girls had carefully selected two new, bigger shells for the crab to choose from, and then they waited and waited for the crab to change houses. When the crab had finally crawled out of the old shell, it was shockingly naked, pink and soft. There was nothing to protect it. Deet felt like that crab without a shell, exposed and vulnerable.

Every car they passed, every person on the street, looked like an enemy, someone who would turn against Dad, against them. The respectable people, the thoughtless people, who wouldn't ask questions, how and why and what sort of person Dad was. They'd just condemn him. A dark town they were living in, full of hard people. Deet wondered why he hadn't seen it before. He wished they could all move away, somewhere else, and never see this town again.

Every house they passed with brightly lit windows made him more bitter. No one in these houses had any worries, they were all happy. They were all free, without a care in the world. And Dad was locked up, like a rabid dog, or something worse.

Deet told the girls not to talk about Dad in school.

Deet wasn't worried about Jam, but P. J. was likely to blab anything to anyone. He felt bad giving them that warning, because he knew that by doing so he'd given them the idea that there was something to be ashamed of.

It was very hard to get out of the car and walk into the school. It was like a grade-school nightmare, like when you were playing Red Rover or something and you were afraid no one would choose you. Or maybe they'd turn and say, *Get out, we don't want to play with you.* What did he care about any of these kids, anyway? What did he care what they thought?

Mom threw him a look of understanding when he got out of the car, but she didn't say anything. It occurred to him that one of the good things about her was that she never said anything stupid, never said anything like, *You'll feel better tomorrow,* or *It could be worse.*

In the school hallway he felt so unprotected that he took all his books out of his locker, instead of just the one he needed for first period. It was as if the big stack of books could make a shield for him.

He walked to Mr. Hodges's class to turn in his homework. He didn't know if people were looking at him funny or not because he didn't look at anyone, just looked straight ahead and tried not to notice anything. He felt angry at every kid in the hall, angry because nothing ever went wrong for any of them, angry because they had such golden lives, angry because they didn't even know anything about life, angry because they had stupid laughs and screechy, horrible voices.

He'd imagined a hundred times what Mr. Hodges would say to him, or what kind of look he'd give him. Mr. Hodges knew Dad because he always took his car into Dan's garage. Mr. Hodges's dad and Dan had been mechanics together, long ago. Deet was proud that Mr. Hodges's dad had been a mechanic too, for some reason, like it gave them something in common. And Dad thought Mr. Hodges was a great guy, especially because Mr. Hodges had bragged about Deet to him, had told Dad that Deet should plan on college when he graduated from high school.

But maybe Mr. Hodges would be embarrassed and wouldn't say anything about Dad, or maybe he wouldn't even have seen the paper.

Mr. Hodges looked up when Deet laid his homework in the basket on his desk. His eyes squinted in sympathy.

"I saw the paper," he said. "Charley."

Deet clenched his jaw tighter. A lump had leaped into this throat as soon as Mr. Hodges spoke.

"Hang in there," said Mr. Hodges. "Hang in there. Charley's not the only one ever got in this kind of trouble, for what that's worth." Mr. Hodges searched Deet's face. He leaned forward on his desk. "I used to work there. In the jail. Teaching English. Before they cut all the education classes. It's not as bad as you might think."

Deet looked at the desk. He didn't know what to say.

Mr. Hodges waved his hand in a helpless way.

"I don't mean that the experience isn't so bad. I just mean that jail isn't anything like it is in the movies. It's more like . . ."

Mr. Hodges looked at the ceiling and the windows, trying to find the right word.

"Boot camp," he said suddenly. "Of course, you've never been in the army, so that wouldn't mean much to you. It's not really like boot camp," he said, seeming to be in despair at trying to describe it, "but anyway, it's not like those stupid jail movies you see. At least not in a little town like this. We haven't got a big enough population to have a lot of bad guys in our jail. Mostly just penny-ante stuff, you know."

He looked at Deet again to see if he'd made any sense. Deet swallowed, wanting not to talk because of the lump.

"Well, I'll shut up about it," said Mr. Hodges. "Just come and see me if you get down."

Deet nodded sadly at Mr. Hodges and left the room. He felt ashamed. Mr. Hodges thought he was a nicer person than he really was. Mr. Hodges thought Deet was only worried about Dad in jail. He was glad Mr. Hodges hadn't known how selfish Deet's first thoughts were, how embarrassed he was for himself. And Mr. Hodges was as upset for Deet, and for Dad, as he could be. Mr. Hodges was hurting for them.

That was something.

He went to sit in his usual seat in the back row of homeroom. He dreaded homeroom more than anything.

He knew how it would be. Someone in the front would glance back at him, and they'd bend over to whisper in their neighbor's ear.

Before he'd opened his book to read, Nelly sat down next to Deet, tilted back his chair against the wall, and folded his arms across his chest. A stern new look had settled on Nelly's face as he watched their classmates. He was ready to protect Deet.

Deet felt a hot wave of affection for Nelly.

He looked at Nelly sideways. "Hi, Nell." His voice sounded odd because it was almost the first time he'd spoken all morning.

Nelly nodded to him gravely. "Hi, Deet," and returned to his surveillance.

And that was another something.

NINE

Everything got easier, just like

people always told you. It got easier every day for
Mom to walk up to those cold steel doors at the jail,
and it took less courage, just a little less, for Deet to
go to school, even when he was back riding the bus.
The knot in his stomach eased up, and he began to eat
again. It had seemed as if he'd never be hungry again,
and his pants were all loose at the waist, but he got his
appetite back.

After the first week in jail, Dad began to call them at
night when he could get to use the phone. Somehow
he managed to make the girls feel like he was all right,
just disgusted with himself. "Daddy says he was an
idiot!" Jam announced delightedly when he'd hung up
after the first call.

Dad could use the phone for only five minutes, so

he usually spent that time talking with the girls. He saw Mom every day, and he knew she'd pass on everything to Deet. Only once did he ask to speak to Deet.

"The kids at school ever say anything to you?" Dad asked in a tight voice.

"Never," said Deet. "Never."

It was true, and Dad could tell it was true by the way he said it.

"Good," said Dad, and he sounded relieved. "That's good. I was worried about that."

No one *had* said a word to Deet about Dad. He didn't know if it was kindness or ignorance. Maybe they didn't read the police column, maybe they hadn't heard. Maybe the cold, blank look on his face was scaring them, maybe he was so unimportant it wasn't worthwhile making him miserable. Maybe Nelly really did keep them away, at least for homeroom and lunch, and the math and PE classes he had with Deet.

But *some* of them knew. Deet could tell.

His math teacher, Mr. Ellis, who was usually sort of distant, treated him differently somehow, seemed more aware of him, looked at him more often or something.

Deet wondered if they'd been talking about Dad in the teachers' lounge.

And once in science, Saul Hastings was goofing around before class and he broke a beaker. Mr. Zingle gave Saul a detention, and one of the other boys had said, in a dramatic voice, "You're going to jail." Immediately Sarah Smith, who sat next to Deet, slid her eyes toward Deet in alarm, obviously upset that someone had said "jail" in front of him. So Sarah knew.

Mom had to get a job. Everything was going to take a long time—the hearings, the trial, the sentencing—and they needed money. She could easily get a waitress job again, she thought. She'd had a lot of experience, and she was good and fast. Deet knew she'd been liked as a waitress because she was happy-go-lucky, chatted with all the customers, and laughed a lot. That's why she'd made so much in tips.

Deet didn't think she would be like that this time. She had become quiet, and he hadn't heard her laugh for a long time.

One night she was late after she'd been to visit

Dad, and when she got home she told them that she'd found a job. "I stopped at the Sourdough Café where I used to work when you were little. Al said he didn't need anyone, but he said he knew they needed someone at Gina's Diner, so he called the owner, Guy Davis, and told him about me, and Guy said to come right over, so I went there and he hired me right away. Al told him I had a lot of experience and I'm good. And fast. They like you to be fast."

On her first day at work, Deet and the girls couldn't help staring at her. She looked so different in her uniform. Trim, neat, efficient, her hair pulled back. Her face scrubbed. She looked older and younger at the same time. Deet was afraid that when she went to work she'd feel like she had at the jail, ashamed and embarrassed. Like he'd felt the first days at school. All the people who came into a diner looking at you. He wished he could get a job instead. He wished he could protect her from people's eyes.

One night he asked her, "When you're at work, do you feel like everyone's looking at you funny?"

She sat down at the table with him and gave a big

sigh. She looked pretty tired. "Well," she said, "I know a lot of people who eat there and a lot know Dad from the shop. First thing I always think is, whoever comes in, I wonder if they know about it. But you wouldn't believe how many people ask me about Dad right away, not even embarrassed, and start telling me about their boyfriend or brother or even themselves getting in trouble. Like I just joined some kind of club."

"Like Sally," said Deet.

"Right. Like Sally. I don't know if I'd want to tell someone stuff like that."

She shook her head, looking a little bewildered. "It's begining to seem as if there are more people who've messed up than ones who haven't. Anyway, when people say things like that to me, I don't feel like we're all alone."

Deet thought about people telling you about their mistakes. They were giving you something very special, weren't they? Like Bingo and Willy, at the shop. When Deet did something wrong, they'd laugh and tell him about something they'd done when they were just starting out.

Nothing could make you feel better than knowing

that someone else had done something stupid too. He'd have to look to see if there was a quote about this.

Every night Mom put all her tips in a glass jar in the cupboard. She said that people who looked like they couldn't afford it would tip the most, but the big-shot guys, especially if there were a lot of them at the table being loud and funny, left the least, sometimes nothing. Tips were the only thing that made a waitress job okay, because they just made minimum wage otherwise. He'd leave big tips when *he* grew up. Huge ones.

It was okay, having Mom working. Deet had to get the girls off to school, which was not a lot of fun, but Mom was home early enough to get supper and go see Dad at night.

But that didn't last long. In a few weeks they changed Mom's shift and things got a lot more complicated. She was working noon to nine, and that meant she couldn't see Dad at all, except on Saturday or Sunday, and there was no help for it.

Deet couldn't stand the idea of Dad being there alone, with no visitors except on weekends.

"Mom," he said, "you've got to let me go visit Dad. He'll go crazy if he doesn't have visitors." He expected a big argument, and part of him was hoping she'd win the argument. But she'd changed her attitude toward the jail, partly from going there every day, and partly from what people had said to her at work.

"I could get the school bus to drop me off in front of the theater, and walk to the jail from there. Then I could get the city bus home an hour and a half later and take care of supper and all, and get the girls to bed."

"What about your homework?" Deet took hours and hours to do his homework. He read the textbooks, underlined them, and then outlined the chapters. He wrote questions for each chapter and then covered the answers with a paper and quizzed himself. He read extra material on whatever they were studying. Whatever the assignment he studied it twice as well as anyone had ever dreamed of. It was a matter of being thorough, and it was a matter of being afraid that he somehow wouldn't remember what was necessary when it was time for the tests.

"I'll have plenty of time to do my homework," Deet

said. He was pretty sure there wouldn't be enough time at all.

"What about the girls? They'll be home an hour before you get here."

"Maybe Sally would let them come there for an hour."

So Mom called Sally, who said she'd be glad to have the girls after school for an hour and to tell Deet that she'd teach him how to cook.

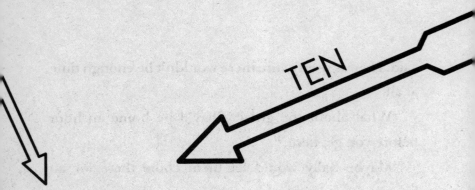

TEN

The next day after school Deet

got off the school bus at the theater. His stomach had been tight all day, thinking about what he had to do. He had a copy of the visiting schedule in his pocket, which he had checked at least three times on the bus, he was so worried about being late.

Deet had never been on the street where the jail was. He crunched past house after respectable house, the old folks' home, a soccer field. A beautiful dog stood on the sidewalk, gravely offering his head to be stroked. Deet bent and gently smoothed the fur on the top of his head. He felt a sudden sorrow for the dog. Being a dog was a lot like being a prisoner. You had to do what you were told, didn't you?

It seemed he'd been walking forever, when he turned a corner and saw it. It was just getting dark, so

Deet's first view of the prison was in a gloomy half light that made it look ominous and chilling. Like a prison movie.

The jail was a big concrete building, and all around it was a chain-link fence, and all around the top of the fence was barbed wire, wrapped in loops. It looked just like the stockades in war movies where prisoners of war were being kept. *Stalag 17*. There were even huge searchlights on a towerlike thing.

It didn't look real. What did he or Dad or anyone else in his family have to do with this movie set?

Deet stopped in the parking lot and stared at the prison, his hands jammed in his parka pockets. He tried to imagine Dad inside there, kept in by all the fences and barbed wire. His mouth felt dry.

Three guards in black uniforms were standing on the front porch, stiff-legged, smoking in jerky puffs because it was so cold. They were all out of shape, bulges of fat hanging over their wide black belts. No gun holsters.

What kind of person becomes a prison guard? (What do you do for a living, sir? Oh, my job is to keep people locked up.) Guards were probably ignorant sorts of people, who smacked their kids around, probably all had fleshy lips and small, mean eyes. People who enjoyed their power over others, like mean teachers who liked to boss little kids around.

Deet walked behind the guards, who didn't give him a glance, and opened the entrance door. He was in a small entranceway. Overhead were vicious-looking little camera eyes and speakers trained down on the people who would gather there. Big Brother is watching you.

Notices and rules were posted everywhere. VISITORS MUST ARRIVE AT THE PROPER TIME. NO ONE WILL BE ADMITTED AFTER THE DOORS ARE LOCKED. VISITORS MUST NOT BRING KNIVES, GUNS, OR CONTRABAND SUBSTANCES INTO THE JAIL.

No *kidding*.

A sign directed him to a button that he could push to enter.

A buzzer sounded and Deet could hear the locks on the door click. He pulled the door open and stepped inside the waiting room, his mouth still dry. He stopped a minute to look around for the registration book Mom had told him about.

The room looked like any public place, shiny white vinyl tiles, fluorescent lights, tan cork bulletin boards filled with notices of some sort. Impersonal, ugly, cold.

There were three doors, two for the bathrooms and another that was behind an arch, a sort of gateway with no gate. A copy machine sat between the two bathroom doors, a water fountain to the right of it. One shabby-looking wooden bench had its back to the copier, and there was a coatrack and a set of dented, short metal lockers in the corner. The paint on the lockers was chipped and dirty.

There was another room behind a glass partition. The floors in there were covered with scruffy-looking carpet, the walls were cement blocks, painted white, and there were chairs, thirty or so, arranged in a semi-circle, facing the glass. A little light came into that room through glass bricks, but there were no windows.

A woman dressed in what looked like a German peasant costume with a full skirt and tight black satin vest was behind the registration window.

She looked up nervously when he approached the window.

"I want to see my dad." Deet's lips were so dry he felt he had to pry them apart to speak.

"Is your dad an inmate?" she asked in a rattled sort of way. She seemed so nervous that Deet was afraid he'd gotten the time wrong, had come to the wrong place.

Deet nodded and gave her his birth certificate, which Mom said he'd have to show to prove that he was old enough to visit by himself. She wrote a number from the certificate in a book on the desk and then pointed to the registration book lying on the counter in front of her.

"Put his name here, your name and address and your social security number." She looked suddenly worried. "Do you know your social security number?"

Deet nodded, feeling insulted. He'd known his social security number since he was *five,* since he'd known there were such things as social security numbers.

Deet filled in the next line on the book in his careful printing. The names on the lines above his were written carelessly. He saw the name of the man who had been arrested before Dad, the first day Deet had looked in the paper for Dad's name. He'd had a visitor today.

Before he finished writing there were people behind him waiting to sign in. Deet hung up his parka on the hooks by the lockers and went to sit on the bench, but he worried that the bench wasn't big enough for all the people, so he went to a corner by the lockers and leaned back against the wall, trying to look as if he was at ease.

He didn't look at the guard who stood off to one side, obviously waiting for something. If he didn't look at him, he wouldn't exist.

A young curly-haired guy, squarely built and as short as Deet, came up to stand next to him. He had brown eyes, concerned and sympathetic. He was wearing some kind of work overalls, and his name patch said ANDY.

"How's it going, man?" he asked. Deet smiled back a little. Not much you could say to that question lately. Except *It's going awful*. Deet had an almost uncontrollable compulsion to ask the guy what he was doing there, who he was visiting, what had that person done to get in jail, how long had he been in there. He wanted to ask how he could stand to be here.

Andy had the air of someone who had been here a lot and would know what was going on, so Deet gestured toward the room behind the glass wall.

"What's that room?"

"That's the contact visit room," Andy said. "A few days every week you can go in there for a visit, and there's no glass between you."

Deet nodded. Mom had told him about contact visits. She hadn't had one yet, because there was a lot of paperwork to go through before you were allowed a contact visit. A lot of checking to see if you were a trustworthy person and all that.

Deet looked at the other people who had signed in. He never paid much attention to people ordinarily, but here he seemed to be overcome with curiosity.

An old woman and an old man, both trim and neat, their white hair silky and smooth, sat on the bench, their feet primly set side by side. They looked like twins. A fat girl, very pretty, had a fat baby who chortled and crowed at everyone. She carried the baby on her hip facing outward, and the baby spun a thin thread of drool onto the floor, while his mother talked to everyone in the room, the guard, the gray-haired couple. This was not a horrible experience for her. She was completely at home here.

The woman behind the glass window dashed out and announced with a little flutter of her fingers, "You can go in now."

Andy jerked his head at Deet to show him to follow.

"Not too many today," he said. "Eight people are allowed to have visitors, because there are only eight phones. Actually there are nine phones, but the one phone has never been fixed ever since I've been coming here."

Deet, the old couple, Andy, and the fat girl with the baby. That meant only four prisoners would have a visit. His mom said the jail was overcrowded, people sleeping in the gym because the prison was designed for a hundred people and there were a hundred and fifty there now. So where were all their visitors?

Everything was so different from the way he'd imagined it that Deet felt confused.

Nobody looked the way Deet thought they would, full of meanness or tragedy. It wasn't like a big drama, it was like normal life, except there was a guard who didn't look anything but a little bored. The only really out-of-the-ordinary thing was the woman behind the registration desk. He'd been disappointed a lot of times in his life when something wasn't the way he thought it would be. Like the circus, which had turned out to be a tawdry affair, the costumes dirty, the acrobats and clowns tired and strained. But this was the first time he'd expected something to be terrible and it was just ordinary.

They entered a long, narrow room made of cement blocks, like the rest of the jail. A long, smeared steel counter divided the room, and a sheet of glass divided one side of the counter from the other. A row of metal stools were bolted to the floor every two feet, and for each stool there was a phone with a long, coiled cord. Deet took the first stool against the wall, but Andy leaned back on his stool and called to him.

"That's the phone that's broken." Deet nodded thanks and moved to a stool in between the old couple and Andy. The glass dividing the counter was smeared and smudged, the floor was littered with bits of tissue and candy wrappers, and under the long glass people had scratched the usual obscenities into the metal frame around the window.

Deet felt uncomfortable that the old couple could see those words.

The metal door on the other side of the glass wall opened suddenly, and a guard let a prisoner into the room. He picked up the phone opposite the old couple and began to talk.

Deet had never seen a prisoner before, and he couldn't help looking from under his eyebrows. He was startlingly handsome, like someone in a movie, and his black hair was as noticeably neat and silken as the hair of the old couple. He looked as if he might be part Eskimo, but the old couple obviously weren't. Maybe his mother or father was Eskimo and these were his grandparents.

You couldn't hear through the glass, but the old woman began to explain why they'd come today instead of some other day, so he must have said something about being surprised to see them. Deet felt embarrassed, listening to a private conversation in such a tight space.

They were a nice little couple, the kind who'd live in those houses on the hill. Were they ashamed to be coming here? What did their prisoner *do*? What was his crime? Their talk was as polite and deliberate as if they were talking over coffee at the kitchen table, not as if they were in a place with bars and locks and guards.

There were two windows on either side of the steel door on the far wall, and Deet could see disorderly lines of prisoners in the same blue suits passing by, looking curiously into the visiting room.

Deet searched their faces to see what could have brought them to jail, but they were so ordinary. Where were the perverts, the steely-eyed hoodlums, the disgusting underbelly of society? They were prisoners, in jail, but they looked like anyone else you might see in the streets. Some were laughing and calling out to each other, just like kids passing from class to class in the halls at school. It was hard to believe the lack of drama in jail. Two prisoners went past the windows dressed in orange suits.

Deet turned to Andy. "Why do some of them have orange suits?"

"That's what you got to wear when you're in seg. Segregation. Means you're being punished for something, like if you got a write-up for something. If you're really, really dangerous you have to wear red."

The guard let in another prisoner, a pretty girl with long orange hair. Her prison uniform was bright yellow. Deet felt a moment of shock and hoped his face hadn't shown it. Somehow he hadn't thought about women going to jail.

She picked up the phone and leaned her face close to the glass to talk to Andy. She was chattering fast, and Andy was just nodding and saying "uh-huh" once in a while. Andy called her Della.

The door clanged open again and a young guy bounced up to the stool opposite the fat girl and the baby, full of good humor.

"Say hi to Daddy," she said, holding the baby up close to the glass. She waved the baby's hand for him.

There was lots of chatter in the room now, so Deet didn't feel like an eavesdropper anymore. The guard popped his head in again and saw Deet sitting without anyone opposite him. He picked up the phone and gestured to Deet to do the same. The phone was so black and greasy-looking, Deet was almost reluctant to pick it up.

The guard's name was on the identification badge clipped to his pocket. TOBOLOWSKY. Mr. Tobolowsky. You probably had to call a guard "mister." He was a thin, slope-shouldered little man with a mild face, so small the big bundle of keys at his hip looked as if it might unbalance him. His name was too big for him as well.

"Who are you visiting?" the guard asked.

"Charley Aafedt," said Deet. Deet felt like Mom had. He'd hated to say Dad's name out loud.

"I'll go get him. Maybe he didn't hear his visitor page," the guard said. He smiled at Deet in a friendly way and left the visiting room. Deet scowled at the metal counter. He thought he would rather have one of those mean-looking guards he had seen when he came in than this guard. It confused him to find a guard so likable.

In a few minutes the door opened and Dad came in. Behind him Mr. Tobolowsky threw Deet a stiff-handed, cheery salute and slammed the door shut again.

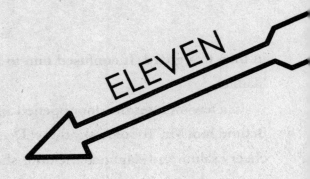

ELEVEN

Dad stood by the door for a

moment, as if he wasn't sure whether he should come into the room or not. He looked shocked to see Deet. Mom must not have told him Deet was coming.

Dad looked very different. Bad. Something about the color of his skin, and the dark places under his eyes. Deet had forgotten how Dad walked, a sort of tipping-forward walk, toed in a little. He had forgotten the way he shook his head back to get his hair out of his eyes.

He sat on the stool opposite Deet and picked up the phone. Dad didn't say anything for a minute. He looked down at his hands spread limply on the counter, and Deet could see he was trying to get himself under control.

"You don't look like you got much sleep," said Deet.

Dad shook his head. "Hard to sleep in here." Dad rubbed his free hand over his hair and stared at the grimy steel counter on his side of the glass.

"I can't believe I let you in for this. I can't believe my kid has to visit me in jail."

Deet was quiet for a minute, listening to the fat girl and the baby, the murmur of the old couple asking what sounded like polite questions, and Andy talking to his girlfriend, telling her the troubles he was having with his car. Ordinary conversations. Nobody was having a hard time like he and Dad were.

Dad still didn't look up. "She said she wasn't going to let you come."

"She doesn't think it's so bad here now. Not as bad as she thought at first."

Dad looked up at that, startled, and gave a little snort.

Deet thought it might be better to change the subject.

"The girls are fine," he said, though Dad hadn't asked how they were. "It's a pain in the butt to get them ready for school. I'm glad I don't have to do it anymore." He mimicked their voices and waggled his head. "This shirt is the wrong color. I don't like this peanut butter. I need money for the book fair." Stupid. He shouldn't have mentioned money.

Dad smiled sadly.

"And I'm learning to cook," said Deet.

He was having trouble finding things to talk about. Dad didn't want to hear him rattling on about stuff like this.

Dad had on the blue prison uniform, a short-sleeved cotton top with a V-neck and baggy blue cotton pants. The uniform looked more like pajamas than regular clothes. The T-shirt underneath was supposed to be white but it was bluish, like it had been dyed in the wash. And dumb-looking canvas slip-ons, the kind tourists wore in the summer.

Those shoes really bothered Deet, they were so lame. It was like Dad wasn't a man anymore with those shoes on. Dad had worn just boots all his life, leather work boots.

There was something about the whole uniform that was humiliating. Powerless. Deet had never thought about clothes before, but he could see now that they made a difference.

"I'll bet you hate those shoes," said Deet.

Dad threw him a grateful look. "You got that right." He looked with disgust at his feet. "These are prison shoes. You can wear your own shoes if you order them through the commissary. You can't bring any in because they think you'll smuggle drugs in in the heels or something, so you have to order them. Smuggling is the big threat in here."

"You going to order some?"

"No," Dad said curtly. "I'm not spending any money while I'm in here. I guess I wouldn't be here if I'd learned not to buy things I didn't need."

The fat girl's baby was screaming with delight, smacking his little palms against the glass, while his dad on the other side of the glass smacked back. He looked as delighted as the baby did. The girl was having a hard time holding the phone as the baby lurched forward more and more recklessly to pound the glass.

It was getting a lot louder in there, and hotter,

almost steamy. The old couple were still talking quietly and courteously to their prisoner, but Andy was talking louder and louder to be heard above the noise of the baby. His girlfriend, or whatever she was, Della, was standing up while she was talking, restless, twirling the phone cord and looking over her shoulder at the prisoners passing by in the hall outside the visiting room.

Suddenly she dropped the phone and darted to the window to pound on it as a group of women prisoners passed by. She shouted something at them. Deet could almost hear her through the glass, she was so loud. Then the girl gestured urgently to the guard watching the women pass, and he came to the door and opened it. The guard waited for her impatiently while she ran to the phone again and explained something to Andy. Then she bounded out to join the other girls, and the door shut behind her.

Deet looked at Andy with surprise. Andy shook his head.

"I took my lunch hour two hours late so I could come see her, and she wants to go play volleyball with the girls." He said the last few words in a little high, mincy voice. He twirled the stool around and stood up. "See ya," he said to Deet cheerfully, and nodded to Deet's father. He went to the door and pushed the signal button. He waited a minute until the locks clunked, then he opened the door and left the room.

Deet turned back to his father. The baby was still making a lot of noise, so he didn't feel too uncomfortable asking the question he couldn't hold back.

"What did *she* do?" he asked.

Dad shrugged an *I don't know*. Then he leaned so close to the glass that the mouthpiece of the phone bonked against it. He made a sort of tent over the mouthpiece with his hand so he couldn't be overheard on his side of the glass.

"Most of the women in here are here for drugs or drunk driving, shoplifting, bad checks." He stopped to think a minute. "Or domestic abuse."

Deet looked blank, so his Dad said, "For beating someone up, you know, like their husband or boyfriend." Dad half-smiled at the look on Deet's face.

"I know, you don't think of women doing things like that." Dad shook his head. "But it's just hard to imagine *anyone* getting so uptight that they want to hit the people they live with. Actually hurt them."

"A few of those women who walked by were old. With gray hair. They looked like *grandmas*," said Deet.

"I guess you never thought old people could get in trouble, huh?" said Dad. "I guess I never did either. There are lots of old people in here. Some of them have been in and out dozens of times. One old guy told me he's spent most of his life in jail."

It reminded Deet of detention at school. There were always the same kids in there, week after week. It had seemed so odd to him that they never learned, never wanted to stay out of there in the worst way. And come to think of it, none of them seemed ashamed, the way Deet would have been if he got a detention. It was ordinary to them, as ordinary as it was to these guys to be in jail.

Deet lowered his voice.

"What's it like in there?"

Dad thought a minute.

"Crowded," he said. "I used to think *our* house was

too small. Now it seems like more room than anyone could ever use up. There's eight of us in this one cell, just a little space, about as big as the laundry room at home. Double bunks and a little space in the middle. So all you can do all day is sit in your bunk. If you need anything, you have to call out through this hole in the door. Like if you want a pencil sharpened or something, you stick it through the hole. There's a toilet in there too, behind a little partition. That's all. Couple of times a day you can leave, going to meals and to the gym, showers."

Dad turned his hands over and looked at the palms. "Look how clean my hands are. I don't think they've been this clean since I was a little kid."

Deet had known there was something else strange about Dad, and that was it. He didn't have grease under his fingernails or in the cracks of his palms.

Dad looked back up at Deet. "You know, I used to think everyone in jail was a bad guy. But there are some nice guys in here, regular guys, like anyone. There's me, and these seven others in our cell. They were really nice to me when I came in, explaining things, loaning me stuff.

"There are two Indian guys from different villages, came into town for the dog races, got drunked up, got in a fight. They won't be in long, not that they seem to care how long it is. They're so cheerful you'd think jail was a Sunday school picnic."

Dad always said that about a Sunday school picnic, as if that was the most mellow thing he could think of. But Deet had once been at a Sunday school picnic with Sally, and it had been a pretty crabby affair, especially after it had started to drizzle.

"Then there's Ben, the bunk under me. Young guy. But this is his zillionth time being in here. He's been busted for everything there is—assault, drunk and dis-orderly, drugs, vandalism, you name it. He can't seem to stay out of the place. I don't know why. He gave me a couple of books to read, otherwise I would have gone crazy just lying on the bunk all day."

Deet tried to picture his dad reading. He'd never seen him read anything but the newspaper. Deet used to think he could read all day if he had a chance, but once he did, and it made him feel half-sick and woozy. He had a hard time getting back to reality when he finally came up for air. It was a very odd feeling.

"Send me some books, will you? You have to mail them. Smuggling rules again."

Deet nodded okay. He was already thinking about what he'd send Dad. Steinbeck. Maybe the Hobbit books. No, not the Hobbit. You had to have a little experience reading before you read something like that. You didn't have to imagine much to read Steinbeck.

Dad counted off his cellmates on his fingers. "There's a black guy, the bunk on top of me. He's the oldest one there. Real quiet and gentle. He just plays solitaire all day on his bunk. Doesn't say much."

Deet was imagining this jail cell like one of those old war movies, where there's one soldier of every race and religion in the squadron, so at the end all the guys can be brothers.

"And then there's Ronny Joseph. He's about as old as me, but he's been in jail most of his life. Started when he was twelve and in juvenile detention. That sounds really bad, doesn't it? But I think he's the nicest guy I ever met."

Dad switched the phone to the other ear, and Deet did the same. His ear felt hot and red, as if he'd been pushing hard on the phone receiver.

"They let us go out for half an hour to walk around the gym at night. Just walk. We can't play in there or anything because they're so overcrowded they have prisoners sleeping in there, mattresses all around the walls. Ronny was walking around with me in the gym last night, telling me about his life. He's part Alaskan Indian, but he wasn't raised here. His mom took him to California when he was a baby. She left him and he was raised in foster homes there, one worse than the other. One jail sentence after another. He said this time was different, though. He has a little girl now, and he wants to make a good life from now on. No drugs, no alcohol. He wants her to have a good family like he never had. I know he'll do it too. Ronny has this sympathy for everyone in here, no matter what they've done. Understanding."

Deet had never seen Dad look so intense, so concerned. "I know I had it pretty easy all my life. I mean Grandpa was tough to get along with and all, but you wouldn't believe what kind of life these guys had when they were little. I can't even tell you all of it. I'd be sick telling you the things they've had done to them. And sometimes when they're telling this stuff they cry, just like they were still little kids."

Dad shook his head slowly. "I never knew stuff like that went on. I've really been sheltered, and that's the truth. I see how easy I had it. Just having fresh air and being outdoors all my life, that's more than most of these guys had. They treat me like I'm a kid, in a way, because I've never been in jail before, never did drugs before, and they say they know I'll never come back over and over like they did. And they don't feel jealous of me, like you'd think, they just wish me well. You wouldn't think you'd meet people like that in jail, would you?"

Dad had entered a whole new world, a world they never knew existed, and he was finding it very interesting. It was making him think new things, look at his life in a different way. That was not something any of them had expected to happen when Dad went to jail.

Deet wished he could see Ronny Joseph. And the rest of the guys in Dad's cell.

When he was on the bus going home, Deet thought about all the things that Dad had told him, and it occurred to him: Dad had been talking like people in a book.

TWELVE

On Deet's next visit the woman

at the desk was wearing tights with thick fluorescent green ankle socks and Nike trainers. A long T-shirt hung almost to her knees, and she had a sweatband on, as if she was going to go out running at any minute. Her clothes were bold and startling, but she herself seemed nervous, as if she didn't want to be noticed. It was really odd.

Andy was there again, but the other visitors Deet hadn't seen before.

One of them was a pleasant-looking young woman with a girl a little younger than P.J.

"When can Daddy come home? What's Daddy doing in here? Why can't he come with us?" she asked her mom, twisting around one of the uprights that formed the entranceway to the visiting room.

Deet thought the mother might be embarrassed to have her little girl ask something like that in public, but the mother answered cheerfully, didn't try to hush the little girl or speak softly herself.

"Well, you know when you do something wrong, you have a time-out? Well, Daddy did something wrong and he's having a time-out."

The little girl nodded gravely and went on twisting herself around the pole.

Andy smiled. He bent over and whispered in Deet's ear, "Good explanation."

There were lots of kids visiting that day. A tight-lipped, gray-haired woman had brought two kids, about eight and ten, Deet guessed. The kids looked at home in the waiting room, as if they'd been visiting the jail for a long time.

The oldest, a boy, sat down beside Deet and looked at him with frank curiosity. "Who are you visiting?" he asked Deet.

"My dad."

The boy nodded. "We're visiting my mom. She was arrested for embezzling."

"Oh," said Deet, feeling a little shocked. Embezzling sounded like a pretty sophisticated crime. Sort of pre-meditated. Now it was his turn to tell what Dad was in for. Why couldn't he be as up-front as this kid? Why couldn't he just say, *Oh, bummer, embezzling. My dad was busted for drugs. My dad was arrested with metham-phetamines. My dad* . . . Forget it. He couldn't say *any-thing* like that, so he asked, "Will she be here long?"

"Two more months. Embezzlement is a white-collar crime and it has a presumptive sentence."

Deet tried to look as if he knew what the boy was talking about.

"That's my grandma, and that's my sister Meghan."

"What's *your* name?" asked Deet, for something to say.

"Ian Foster Carmichael," the boy said, chin up and eyes bright. Having a mom in jail hadn't damaged *his* self-image, Deet thought. Meghan looked like Jam—long, wispy blond hair, brown eyes, fidgety. In her hair was a purple plastic barrette that she'd obviously been adjusting herself, because it was crooked and the hair was bunched up under it. Deet wished the grandma would unclasp it, brush down Meghan's hair, and put it back in right.

The last visitor to come in was a tall, wild-haired black woman with a little boy, maybe two years old, on her hip. After she'd taken off his snowsuit, he was all over the waiting room, his mom loping after him, calling out commands he ignored. "Michael, sit your sorry ass down in this chair!"

He was so fast and his mom was so gangly that Deet felt himself laughing, for the first time since Dad had been sent to jail.

Andy picked up the little boy so she could sign in, throwing him high in the air over his head, making him shriek with laughter. Andy was the kind of person who saw what was needed and did it.

Deet could see it was going to be really noisy today, locked in that little room with all those kids. That was good, because the more noise there was, the less uncomfortable he felt.

When it was time to go into the visiting room there was a different routine. A guard stood in front of the archway before they went in and waved a wandlike thing over them, up and down on both sides, to check for metal or something.

This guard was tall and must have been an athlete, because he had the most perfect build Deet had ever seen outside of the movies. He was triangle-shaped, like a GI Joe doll. He had a lighthearted way of dealing with everyone. Kind eyes. Deet was afraid he was staring at him as he watched him run the wand over everyone, making it funny. Deet had never thought there would be nice guards, and here was another besides Mr. Tobolowsky.

Dad looked worse than ever. His skin was stretched tight across his cheekbones, his nose seemed sharper, and his eyes were pinched-looking or something.

Deet took the stool against the wall, which he thought might not be so noisy. When Dad picked up the phone, Deet said, "They searched us this time with a metal detector thing."

"Yeah, last night they had a big fight in here, on the visitors' side. Two women got into it, and one of them had a pocketknife. I think they both came to see the same guy." Dad smiled.

Good thing Mom didn't know about that, or she might not have let him come.

"There was a fight in our cell last night too," Dad said.

"Wow," said Deet, thinking about how small the cell was, wondering how they'd found room to fight.

"We got two new guys in there, and they got into it. Over a *towel,* if you can believe it. I thought I'd seen fights before, but I never saw anything like this. Worse than anything I ever saw in the movies. Ronny got right in there and broke it up, talking fast, and he got them calmed down. But not before there was blood everywhere. The smell of blood and sweat in that little room—I thought I was going to be sick.

"Then the guards came and they made us all get out of the cell and go to the gym because they had to clean the blood up. They worry about AIDS anytime there's blood. We didn't get to sleep until after midnight."

This was the kind of thing Deet had thought about when Dad first went in. Violence. And here he'd just begun to think that jail was not so bad, and that all the inmates were easygoing.

"What happens to guys who fight?"

"They put them in seg for a while. They have a hearing to see whose fault it was. I saw both of them today and they were wearing orange suits." He shook his head. "To tell you the truth, I think something was wrong with that one guy. He didn't look like he was all there. Ronny says they get a lot of crazies in here, you know."

"What would they put someone like that in jail for? Don't they put them in a hospital or something if they're crazy?"

"No," said Dad. "There are lots of guys in here who need a psychiatrist more than they need to be locked up. Doesn't make any difference to the law *why* you did something."

Michael was all over the visiting room, tugging at Deet's shirt, wanting to get up, running from family to family, trying to get someone to play with him. And Michael's mom was darting here and there with the phone in one hand, trying to rein him in. His dad was tall too, and he was getting a kick out of Michael's antics.

Andy was arguing with his girlfriend about an apartment she wanted to rent when she got out. She was wearing a lot of makeup and had spent a lot of time on her curly red hair.

Meghan and Ian were taking turns on the phone, talking to their mother, who looked just like anyone you'd see in a store—a bank clerk, a saleswoman. Their grandmother leaned against the back wall, maybe waiting for her turn on the phone, looking pretty sour. Deet wondered if she was mad at her daughter for getting thrown in jail. Looked like it.

"I sent you some books today. Mom mailed them this morning," said Deet.

Dad nodded his thanks. "Send me some of my old motorcycle magazines, will you?" he asked. "For Ronny."

"Sure," said Deet. He felt pleased to be doing something for Ronny. He liked hearing about Ronny more than anyone else Dad talked about. "What about sending you some cassette tapes or CDs?"

"They stopped letting guys listen to music before I got here. Too much stuff gets smuggled in with cassette tapes, I guess. And some part of the cassette player was being used to make illegal tattooing needles."

Deet didn't know what to make of that. "CD players, too?"

"Yeah, them too." Dad shook his head. "It's kind of interesting, the things people can come up with in here to relieve the boredom. You have to hand it to them, it's kind of ingenious. They shut the hobby shop down yesterday too. No funding. They used to have classes and stuff for the prisoners, but those are all shut down too."

"In all the prison movies you can go to school in jail and get a degree and everything."

Dad rolled his eyes. "Not here."

Dad was quiet for a minute, watching Michael zoom around the visiting room. Deet wondered if he was thinking about P. J. and Jam when they were that age.

"We got another new guy in the cell today. He's had a lot of trouble. He says all he wants out of life now is to have a house and a dog. He says he's too old to get married or have kids, but he'll be happy if he can have his own house. And a dog. Doesn't seem like much to ask for out of life, does it?"

Deet could see an old guy sitting on the steps of a small white house, a shaggy old dog by his knee, both of them looking at the sunset. Deet felt sad thinking about someone who dreamed about the ordinary things everyone took for granted, as if they were unbelievably precious.

They talked about the truck, which would be impounded until Dad was sentenced, and about the guys at the shop. Willie and Dan had come to visit him. Dan said it was no problem to just carry him on the payroll so the insurance would still be valid. He said he didn't need to hire anyone to take Charley's place. Everyone had said they'd work a little longer every day to make up for it. Charley wouldn't be in jail long enough to worry about it, Dan said. It already seemed like a very long time to Deet.

Michael's mom had had enough of trying to nail him down, and she grabbed him up and headed for the button by the door. Michael's dad lounged over to the door, making conversation with the rest of the prisoners behind the glass, joking about his son, it looked like. They all laughed.

Andy slid off his stool and blew a kiss to Della. "Well, I got to get back to work," he said. She wiggled her fingers good-bye and flounced to the door to wait for a guard to let her out. Ian and Meghan's grandmother was talking to her daughter now, speaking quietly, reluctantly. Deet was sure she didn't want to be there.

The woman with the running outfit stuck her head in the door. "Time's up," she said, looking as if she was afraid someone would quarrel with her.

Deet hung up his phone and started to the door, looking back over his shoulder at Dad, standing in the other half with Meghan and Ian's mom, Michael's father, and Andy's red-haired girlfriend. Ordinary enough people, talking, having a laugh, waiting for a guard to unlock the door for them. Criminals.

THIRTEEN

Mom's new schedule made a

lot more work for Deet, but having so much to do kept him from worrying so much.

He worried a lot—about money, about the trial, about Dad's health—and he worried about the corners he was cutting with his schoolwork. Anytime Deet worried, he'd make a list. Two sides: good points and bad points, sure things and unknown things. He was very analytical.

Deet worried about forgetting something important in the daily chores, so he made a carefully printed list of things to do.

In the morning Mom took care of breakfast and did the breakfast dishes before she went to work. She got the girls ready for school because she didn't go to work until noon.

That was one reason Deet didn't mind this new schedule, even though he had so much to do. Getting the girls ready for school was the part he'd hated. It made him crazy, worrying that they'd be late, that their hair wasn't right, that they'd forget something they needed.

And then there was homework, which the girls would forget until the last minute, or which they'd whine and whimper over, or their library books, which were always late and hiding in the most unlikely places.

And there were buttons that had to be sewed on, and things replaced that were lost, like P. J.'s gym sneakers and Jam's mittens. There was no end to it.

He might be able to take care of the house and all, but he wasn't much in the mother line.

Mom did the shopping, too, which she had to do because Deet couldn't drive; she did the laundry; and she cooked on Saturday and Sunday. Deet did the rest.

He pinned the list on his bulletin board, a tack on each corner so it wouldn't curl.

2:30–3:00: Bus to jail
3:10–4:10: Visit Dad

4:10–4:30: Catch the bus

4:30–5:00: Bus home

5:00: Get P. J. and Jam

5:15–6:15: Cook dinner, girls fold laundry if
there's any

6:15–6:30: Eat dinner

6:30–7:00: Make lunches, girls clean up toys,
see if girls have homework

7:00: Girls take baths while I wash dishes,
vacuum the house

7:30–8:00: Read a story

8:00–10:00: Do my homework

6:00: Get up

6:45: Catch bus

Saturday and Sunday: Mop the floors, dust,
clean the stove, refrigerator, clean the
bathroom, etc.

He wrote "etc." because he wasn't quite sure what
other things needed to be done once a week, but he
was sure there must be some.

It was a tight schedule, because visiting Dad took

a lot of time. But it was the most important thing on that list, because Dad was locked up in that tiny cell, and just to walk down to the visiting room was a big deal.

The main thing Deet wanted to do was to clean out all the drawers and closets and cupboards. The thing that was wrong with their life was those cupboards and stuff. They set the tone for the way their life was lived. He'd get them so neat, so perfectly organized, that they'd be able to find everything in an instant.

He started with the kitchen cupboards. It took him until midnight one night. He scrubbed every cupboard out, lined the shelves with foil, organized things sensibly. All the baking things were together, all the cooking things together. He threw out a zillion nearly empty ketchup bottles and toothpick boxes and consolidated three baking soda boxes into one. There was a lifetime supply of papery onion skins in the vegetable bin, and three rotten potatoes oozing foul-smelling, putrid fluid. He wanted to throw out all the chipped dishes, but he had to reconsider because he was afraid they wouldn't have enough to eat on if he did.

Deet was gaining a new respect for housework now that he'd done it for a while. He'd always hated it that their house was messy and disorganized. But he was beginning to see that there was more to being unmessy and organized than met the eye. He looked up quotations about housework after a particularly frantic night when there seemed to be too many things to do and too little time.

There is scarcely any less bother in the running of a family than in that of an entire state. And domestic business is no less importunate for being less important.
—MONTAIGNE

Deet had to look up "importunate." It meant troublesomely urgent. That was the right word, all right. Everything had to be done *now*, and nothing could be left out. If you didn't do the laundry, no one would have clothes for school. If you didn't make a list of menus, you wouldn't get what you needed at the store and you wouldn't have what you needed to cook dinner and make lunches. And you wouldn't have the meat thawed. If you didn't get the house cleaned up at night, you'd be in a mess in the morning.

He could find only one more quotation about housework.

MRS. PRITCHARD: *I must dust the blinds and then I must raise them.*

MRS. OGMORE-PRITCHARD: *And before you let the sun in, mind it wipes its shoes.*

—DYLAN THOMAS

Deet wrote both quotations in his notebook and then doodled on his desk pad for a few minutes, thinking about housework. He remembered that they were out of Scotch tape, so he made a new list for Mom, Things to Buy on Saturday. He wrote "Scotch tape" under that, and then he jumped up to stick the list on the refrigerator, under Jam's Elmo magnet.

Then he started to write.

There were only these two quotations about house-work in the quotation book.

That seems really funny, because everyone has a house, or a place to live, and someone has to clean that place, and do the laundry and wash the dishes and take care of everything, so it's a very important subject, isn't it? But hardly anybody has said anything famous about it.

Maybe that's because the people who say things that become famous quotations didn't do their own housework. Just Montaigne. You can tell he did. Whoever he was.

When you do housework, there are a lot of things you do that no one notices. Nobody says, oh, you vacuumed the floor, or you washed out the tub, unless the rug and the tub were so grungy that anyone would notice an improvement. Our house was always messy, but I never noticed that it was always clean. I just noticed that there was stuff all over, not put away neatly.

Now that I'm doing the housework since my mom went back to work, I can see all the things I didn't notice before. You can clean out the refrigerator all you like, but all the other people in the family are going to mess it up faster than you can blink. I feel really touchy about people messing things up now, so I know what "mind it wipes its shoes" means. This is the job you do, cleaning a house, and people come along at any minute and mess it up. And don't even notice. I actually say things like, "Put that glass away," or "Wipe up that spill." I feel really silly after I've said something like that. My mom was never fussy; she never said things like that when she was cleaning the house.

There are a million people all over the world, billions of people, most of them women probably, who have discovered all this and more about taking care of a house. It's the not noticing that is the worst, I think. What if you tried to talk about what you did that day. "I scrubbed the floor this morning, and was it a mess. Took me a half hour on my hands and knees." The most you'd get would be a look. Not much conversation material in that. No wonder housewives felt unappreciated. No wonder there was women's lib.

Like housework, cooking was a lot more compli-cated than it looked, but it got a lot more comments. One night Deet made that kind of macaroni and cheese that comes in a box, but the next day he asked Sally how to make it from scratch, so they had it again, only this time it was much better, with lots of real cheese melting all over the macaroni. The girls seemed a little surprised to have the same thing two nights in a row. Deet didn't think he'd mind eating the same thing for a *week*, if it was something he liked.

After that Deet got out his mom's recipe box to look for ideas. He decided to make his grandma's famous meatballs. Swedish meatballs. In white gravy. Unbelievably good, they just melted in your mouth.

He had a bad moment when he found that he needed sour cream, but he found some in the refrigerator, way in the back. There was a nasty patch of blue mold on the edge of the carton, but he scraped it off and used the rest.

They were easy to make, Swedish meatballs, but they wouldn't stay balls. They flattened out on him when they cooked. They were almost meat squares. P. J. and Jam didn't think they tasted good because they were the wrong shape. He'd have to ask Sally how to get them to stay round.

But they tasted fine to him, and there was a whole pile of mashed potatoes. He'd ask Sally how to get the lumps out of the potatoes, too.

Deet looked for quotations about cooking. Lots more quotations on food than on housework.

We each day dig our graves with our teeth.
—SAMUEL SMILES

Absolutely. Just what he'd been thinking. All that fat and sugar. And double hamburgers and giant bags of French fries. All those fat people in Kmart, sucking on big Slurpees as they stumbled along behind shopping carts, all the exercise they were going to get in a week.

I never see any home cooking. All I get is fancy stuff.
—PRINCE PHILIP, DUKE OF EDINBURGH

That was the Queen of England's husband. Deet thought about that for a minute. He didn't know enough about fancy food to decide if the duke was missing anything or not. But if mashed potatoes was home cooking, he did feel sorry for the duke. Deet could have lived on mashed potatoes.

Tell me what you eat, and I will tell you what you are.
—BRILLAT-SAVARIN

That was a good one. But it wasn't as easy to write about as it had looked, because Deet found he didn't really know that much about food. He hadn't thought about all the different ways that people eat, and it took some time to think it out. There was hardly time to do his civics when he was finished.

If you were a vegetarian and ate only plants and things you don't have to kill an animal to get, like milk and eggs, this guy would say you were a kind person, a person who cared as much about animals as about himself.
Or maybe it just means that you think animal fat is the thing that causes heart attacks and so

you eat this way to protect yourself. So you would be self-protective, not kind.

If you ate nothing but Hostess Twinkies, like Donny Allen in our class, that would mean you're kind of a baby, really, wouldn't it? All sugar, and not even having to chew hard.

Or if you eat the same things over and over, like my grandma and grandpa, it probably means you're stuck in a rut. My dad says when he was little they even had a schedule: chicken on Sunday, baked beans and hot dogs on Friday, and so on. That's weird.

There's our friend Sally, who's just the opposite. She's always trying something new, usually from some foreign country, like Greece or India. So Sally would be the opposite of stuck in a rut. Adventurous, I guess you'd say.

And Sally says lots of times her experiment is a failure, and she and her husband have to go out and get a hamburger! So I guess you'd say they're not tight about money, either, because it costs a lot to pay for two meals when it was supposed to be only one. If you were stingy, you'd make only things you knew you could eat.

My mom fixed things she thought of at the last minute, and there was always something she didn't have, so I'd always have to run down to Sally's to borrow it. So I guess you'd say the way we ate showed that nobody was thinking ahead.

If you eat only fancy stuff, like a duke, it probably means you're rich. And if you eat only stuff from the supermarket deli, like those guys you see lined up there every night, you are probably very busy and don't have a wife to cook. Or maybe you're not busy, but just lazy. Or maybe you're married, but your wife can't cook.

I'll have to think about this quotation some more, because I really haven't paid much attention to how other people eat.

His schedule wasn't working out so well, because he'd underestimated the amount of time it would take to get the girls to bed. He'd have to be more flexible, he saw. So that night he washed the dishes after he finished his homework. Before he made their lunches for school, he washed the girls' lunch boxes with bleach. They always smelled like something weird. He could never get that smell out of them.

Jam had a Barbie lunch box and P. J. had an Elmo lunch box, and you didn't ever want to get them mixed up. It was not easy making lunches for them, because they complained about everything. Jam wanted honey with her peanut butter, and P. J. wanted jelly, but not grape jelly, just strawberry jelly. And Jam wanted her sandwiches cut in half, and P. J. liked quarters.

The person who cooks takes a lot of flak, Deet was learning.

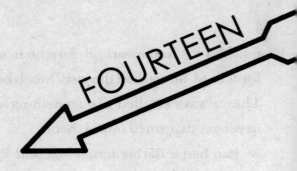

FOURTEEN

When Dad called at night, the

girls would chatter on about school, complain about Deet's cooking, and tattle on each other. Dad managed to make the girls feel he was interested in them, not removed from their lives. In the old days, Deet thought, before there were phones, going to jail must have been like a death in the family.

Dad didn't talk about what was going on with him, he just asked the girls question after question, kept them chattering, and when they were finished they felt close to him. Where had he learned a thing like that? Not from Grandpa or Grandma. They never asked questions, at least not the kind that showed an inter- est, showed you were paying attention. Dad just knew how to make people feel good. It was like the way he knew that sidewise way of giving compliments. The next time Deet had trouble thinking about what to talk about to anyone, he'd just ask questions.

"When can we come to see you, Dad?" P. J. asked every time.

"Not ever," he'd say. "Never. You can't talk in here very well, because there are so many people around. It's better to talk on the telephone." But Deet knew he didn't want the girls to see him in there. You think your dad is the king of the world, you think he can do anything. And then you see him led around by these guards, locked in, locked out, and then you know he isn't the king. Maybe what you don't see you can forget about easier. Maybe if the girls never saw him there, it wouldn't be real to them.

One night Dad told the girls, "Hold the phone up to the speakers and play me something on the CD player. Some Willie Nelson. Anything."

So they played some of his favorite songs for him. "Louder," he said. "Lots louder." They had to turn it up so loud Deet and the girls could hardly stand it. It was noisy in the jail at night, iron gates clanging, people yelling, so Dad couldn't hear it unless it was cranked all the way up.

"Thanks," said Dad. "I can't believe how much I miss my music. Can you find 'The Gambler'? Ronny wants to hear that one. It's on that album with the stars on the front."

P. J. found it right away. She was getting a kick out of playing deejay.

They all liked that one too. "You got to know when to hold 'em, know when to fold 'em," they sang along as loud as they could, feeling joyful.

When the song was finished, Dad said, "Ronny thanks you. He says that's his new theme song, the one he's going to live by."

Know when to walk away and know when to run, thought Deet. *That's what Ronny has to do, all right.*

One day that week Mom had taken a few hours off to go to the dentist, so she said she'd see Dad that day, before her appointment. Deet would take the school bus home instead of the downtown bus and give Sally a day off from the girls.

When he got out of school, Deet was surprised to see that Nelly wasn't waiting for him at their bus station. Usually Nelly was there first, because he had a study hall last period, but he wasn't first that day, and Deet was by himself. He felt his stomach clench a little when he saw Dennis Slater come up.

Dennis was a sort of smart-ass, an arrogant kind of guy, basketball star and all that. He lived on the ridge in one of the last houses on their bus run. Every time Nelly saw Dennis coming, or anyone like him, he'd start talking ninety miles a minute, sort of leaning toward Deet, so no one else could get a word in. So they could ignore everyone, being so absorbed in their conversation. Now here was Dennis, and no Nelly to run interference.

Dennis nodded at Deet, bent down to pick up an ice chunk, and threw it, free-throw style, into a garbage can.

"Slam dunk," Dennis said when the ice thunked on the bottom of the can. Deet gave him a small smile.

Dennis came closer and put both of his hands in his pockets. He was one of those cool guys who didn't wear a hat or mittens, even when it was ninety below. He folded his mouth in a tight line and then he said, "My brother is in there." Deet looked at him blankly. In *where*?

Dennis pushed his hair out of his eyes. "He says your dad is a good guy. They play cards together sometimes."

Jeez, Dennis Slater knew. That about tied it. Dennis wasn't exactly the kind of guy to keep things to himself. Then Deet wondered why Dad never mentioned anyone with a brother in school. Maybe he didn't know.

Well, he had to say something. Ask a question.

"Do you ever go to see him?"

"No," said Dennis. "My mom won't let me." He picked up a bigger piece of ice and made another basket. "I know you go to see your dad. My brother told me he saw you there when he was walking past the visiting room."

"Yeah," said Deet. "I go every school day. Not today, because my mom was off. She goes on the weekends because she's usually working the other days."

"I told my mom you go, so why couldn't I. But she can't see it." Deet felt uncomfortable thinking about this mom and her boy, people he didn't even know, talking about things he thought were private.

"Just my other brother goes. He doesn't live at

home, so he can do what he wants to. I wish I could visit Jerry."

Deet looked at Dennis for a long minute, trying to remember how wary he'd been of guys like Dennis, lippy guys, sure of themselves. Dennis just looked sad now.

"Is he going to be there long?" asked Deet. Not what he'd wanted to say. He wanted to say something to make Dennis feel better.

"Don't know," said Dennis.

Deet nodded. At that moment Mindy pulled their bus into its space by the crossing sign, and at the same time a swarm of kids came from the school, Nelly as well. Nelly looked a dark look at Dennis and moved to Deet's side, ready to interfere. Deet smiled a *don't worry* smile at Nelly.

Dennis said, "How's it going, Nelly?" and then, "See ya," to Deet.

Before Dennis turned away, Deet said to him, "It's not so bad, you know, that place." Dennis looked at Deet for a moment in an I'll-take-your-word-for-it sort of way and went to take his place in the bus line.

After they were on the bus, Nelly and Deet in their

usual front seat behind Mindy, Nelly looked a question at him and Deet said, "His brother's in jail. With Dad."

"No *kidding*," said Nelly.

"There are a lot of surprises in this world," said Deet.

When Deet got his homework back on Thursday he flipped quickly through the pages to see what Mr. Hodges had to say about cooking and housework. He'd written:

> *Some people don't even like to eat, you know. That's because they were raised by the food nazis. Those are the ones who make kids eat everything on their plate, even if they're not hungry or don't like it. The ones who make them try everything. The ones who take it as a personal insult if you say you don't like artichokes or anchovies or almonds. The food nazis are everywhere, feeling righteous, making little kids' meals a battleground and a misery!*

Deet wondered if Mr. Hodges was talking about himself, and if that was why he was so skinny.

And under that Mr. Hodges had written:

What does your dad say about the food in jail?
When I worked there it was awful.

Why hadn't he thought to ask Dad about the food?
What *did* they eat in jail?

When Deet was waiting for the bus home, sometimes
he went into a store that sold used CDs, mostly to stay
warm, but also because he liked it there.

The guys who owned it were cool. Young guys,
kind of far out, earrings and ponytails and T-shirts
with social comments like "What if they gave a war and
nobody came?" and "I feel like a fugitive from the law of
averages." There was a poster by the door that showed
a sleek black leopard, and in the cartoon balloon coming out of its mouth were the words: "Animals are not
fabric. Wear your own damn skin."

One of guys had a great big yellow dog that greeted
you when you came in. They treated that dog as if they
felt the dog had dignity and rights and was a creature

with his own life and plans and needs. The dog was their equal, and there was nothing patronizing about their behavior toward him. Deet liked that.

The guys interested him because they were always putting out petitions and collecting money for causes—the environment, animal rights, equal pay for women, the food bank. Deet had never been around people who were thinking about stuff like that. He wished he could work up the courage to talk to them.

One night there was a blue clipboard on the counter with a list of people's signatures, and a ballpoint pen was tied to the clip. It was a petition to legalize marijuana. Deet stopped and stared at it.

The bus pulled up by the door, and Deet ran outside to catch it. He was thinking about the petition so hard that he barely remembered to give the driver his ticket to punch.

He'd always thought of laws as just being there, never changing. Not open to discussion, petitions. But what if there were no laws against drugs? What if drugs were like alcohol? Or cigarettes? Legal at a certain age. Who decides things like what's right and wrong?

Dad said that nearly everyone in jail was there for drugs. If drugs were legal, most of the people wouldn't be there. What was the use of going to jail, anyway? Did it do any good, even if you were a mugger or something? What if you had to work for the poor or the old, instead of going to jail? What if you just had to pay back the money you stole, or whatever you did?

Grandpa said Dad was going to hell for using drugs. Well, what if drugs weren't against the law? Would the rules for hell change? There used to be a law against alcohol. Grandpa drank sometimes, schnapps and brandy and beer. Would you go to hell back then, during Prohibition, for drinking, but not now when the law said it was okay? (Deet thought hell was just a silly idea anyway, like the bogeyman, supposed to make you scared to do things, but he thought that people who *did* believe in it should at least have logical rules for hell.)

The next day Deet was at the jail before anyone else, so he went to the bulletin board to study the monthly menu he'd seen there. Each meal was huge, and the total of calories per day was listed as four thousand. Wasn't that way too many calories? The menu was overloaded with turkey. There was turkey bacon, turkey sausage, turkey hot dogs, turkey roll, turkey burgers, and turkey patties. What the heck was turkey bacon? And in the old days they used to give prisoners just bread and water.

Deet knew now that the woman at the registration desk was named Rhonda. She was wearing a sort of man's outfit today. A gray man's suit and a man's tie. It looked okay, but it was kind of weird that she had so many styles. What did her closet look like? It must look like a costume store. How did she decide every day who she was going to be?

It seemed to Deet as if a person's clothes should be sort of the same all the time, as if they were telling you with their clothes who they were. Like the kids at school. This one wore only the latest stuff: *I'm* in. *I'm on the cutting edge.* This teacher with the long hair and long skirts said, *I'm into whole wheat and women's rights and environmental issues.* The girls who wore really outrageous stuff to get attention were saying, *Look at me.* Deet's clothes said, Don't *look at me.*

Andy was there again, and so was the fat girl with

the baby. An old black man Deet had never seen before came in. A big, beefy man with a shirt and tie passed through the gate with a large Bible tucked under his arm. In his pudgy hand he had a pass Rhonda had given him, and he waved it at the guard on the other side of the door. Deet wondered what this man told the prisoners he visited about hell.

Deet sat on the bench and listened to Andy, who told Deet all about his job at the parts place. His car was giving him problems, and some days it was hard to get here to the jail to visit, but if he didn't come his Della thought right away that he was fooling around on her, had another girlfriend.

"People get really jealous in here, you know? If she tries to call me and the line is busy, I catch holy hell trying to explain who I was talking to."

Deet wondered if Dad would get jealous. No. Couldn't happen. Neither of his folks were the jealous type.

Just a second before the automatic timer shut the entrance door, a girl rushed in, practically running.

Deet froze on the bench. Sheena Daily. She went

to his school, but he almost hadn't recognized her, because it was so wrong to see her in a place like this. One year they'd been in the same classroom, maybe when they were in the third grade. She'd had long braids and glasses so thick that her long eyelashes mashed up against the lenses. She didn't wear glasses anymore, and her hair was cut short like a boy's.

He wished he could be invisible.

When she had signed in, she turned and saw Deet. She came to the bench and looked down at him. Andy gave her a friendly greeting, so Deet knew he'd seen her visiting before.

"Hi. I guess I won't ask you what you're doing here. I read about your dad in the paper. At least I thought it must be your father. Not too many people have that name. My brother is here. My folks won't come to see him, so I try to come whenever I can."

Deet thought for a minute how he'd almost convinced himself that hardly anyone at school knew. And here were Sheena and Dennis in one week. Then he remembered how he was going to ask questions when he couldn't think of anything to say, but he couldn't think of any questions to ask that wouldn't be rude. (*What did your brother* do?)

He was relieved when Rhonda darted out of the office in her suit. "You can go in now," she said. There was no guard with a wand this time.

The old black man took the stool next to Deet. "Here she come," he chortled to Deet, as a merry-looking girl with honey-colored skin peeked in the window to the visiting room. The old man looked pleased. "Don't never learn, that girl. Busted her parole, I don't know how many times."

The guard, a woman, let the girl in, and she bounced to the stool, casting impudent looks at her father.

"Don't be sweetie-pieing me," he complained. "I'm tired as can be of your foolishment."

Deet couldn't hear what the girl said, but she wasn't afraid of him, that was for sure, and the old man was having a hard time keeping from laughing.

"Don't give me none of your sass," he said to her.

Deet wanted to tell Dad about the petition he'd seen at the CD store, ask him what he thought about it. But he thought it might be kind of dumb to ask a person in

Dad's position what he thought about jailing people for drugs, so he didn't say anything.

Sheena was talking doggedly to her brother, who was not in a very good mood. He looked down at the steel counter the whole time and never looked into Sheena's face. She looked over and caught Deet's eye, smiled sadly, and looked back at her downcast brother.

Deet had never seen this woman guard who was letting the prisoners in. She was short and stocky and she looked angry. She was very young, but she didn't smile at anyone.

"What's *she* like, Dad?"

Dad made a face. "She's scared to death of everyone. She never turns her back on anyone, never relaxes. She scares *me*. Being scared makes people more dangerous than anything. Just like dogs, or bears."

Deet asked Dad about the food, and about what he was reading, and what was new with the other guys in his cell. It was a good trick, asking questions. It filled in all the blank spaces.

Every day Dad had a new story to tell Deet. Sometimes they were funny stories, like the time

Ronny Joseph smuggled oranges out of the dining hall and back to their room. But most of the time they were sad, things people had told him when they were tired of reading and were just shooting the bull.

Sheena got up and put her phone on its hook. Her brother turned his back on her and walked to the door to wait for the guard to open it.

"See you at school tomorrow," she said. She pushed the button and waited for the clunk to signal that it had been unlocked.

"You know her?" asked Dad.

"She's at school with me," said Deet. "Her mom and dad won't visit her brother."

"Like me," said Dad.

That night Deet sat down to answer Mr. Hodges about the food in jail. He thought for a minute about what to write at the top of the page, and then he just wrote "JAIL" in capital letters.

The food in jail is mostly cheap, that's the really important thing. Instead of bacon, they have turkey bacon. And turkey hot dogs, turkey burgers, turkey sausage, and turkey loaf. My dad says for sure he'll never eat turkey again. The inmates work in the kitchen and do the cooking, so it's not exactly home cooking. Dad says a lot of guys gain weight because they don't get any exercise and because the food is so fattening. He's getting skinnier.

My dad said he used to think that people went to jail because they were bad. But he said now he doesn't see how some people can keep from going to jail, given what they've had to put up with, what kind of childhoods they had. Some of them have been in dozens of foster homes, and that's where people are supposed to take extra good care of you to make up for what happened with your parents. He's heard lots of bad stories about foster homes. Well, it's not always like that. Some people who get in trouble come from good homes, but a lot of things can happen to you, like hanging out with the wrong people, or maybe you get to be an addict in a really easy way, you don't think you will but *before you know it you can't live without whatever it is you're addicted to, liquor or different drugs, and then you don't know how to stop. They have classes in there for drugs and alcohol too. My dad has to go to these before he gets out.*

And you can see why people want to steal things. You know you'll never have a car like that, or even a car, period, because you didn't finish school. You know you won't have fancy clothes, or the stuff you see on television, so you take it. It's beginning to look to me as if the world isn't fair. Not even a little bit.

When Deet got that homework back, Mr. Hodges had written a quotation at the bottom of the page.

Poverty and violence, a family life devoid of warmth or order make an education impossible and sociopathy inevitable. Children so cheated, so deprived, cannot rise above the deprivation and will fill our jails. But who are the criminals?

—E. G. WOOD

FIFTEEN

On the next Sunday, one of her

days off, Mom was all business. She had a pile of bills and a yellow pad and pencil in front of her on the table. She was trying to figure out what to pay and what not to pay, and how to pay the lawyer.

Sally had taken the girls ice-skating. She was doing the kind of weekend running around that Deet's mom used to do with the girls before she had to go to work.

Deet had spread the newspaper out over one end of the table and was going over it very carefully, the way he did every day.

First he'd turn to the police reports and then to the court judgments. Now he knew people by name who were in jail, and he wanted to know whether or not they were convicted and what their sentence was.

He noticed which judges gave the most lenient

sentences and which the harshest. He knew all the judges by name. There could be a lot of difference between one judge and another. He hoped Dad would come up before the mellowest one of all. It was Johnson you wanted to stay away from. Andy said he was mean as spit.

He skimmed over the headlines of each article, seeing if there was anything to do with the drug laws, the prison system, or local police business. He read the report of a trial in the States where this judge had thrown the book at a guy he said didn't show remorse. The guy had said he was innocent, so how could he show remorse for something he didn't do? How illogical could you get?

And what would it be like to be innocent and have nobody believe you? It was one thing to go to jail for something you did do, but something else to go to jail for something you didn't do. Like those guys you'd read about in the paper who got out of jail after seventeen years when somebody else admitted to the crime. Or they did a DNA test or something.

Once Deet had thought that what happened to Dad

was the worst thing that could ever happen. Now he knew that there were worse things. Much worse.

Mom sighed. "I just don't know where to start."

Deet folded up the paper neatly and put it in the section of the woodbox he'd made for paper.

He looked at her curiously. Here was Mom, ditzy little Mom, with a calculator and a yellow pad, looking efficient. She was like a whole new person.

Deet had often wished he could take care of the family bills and organize them into a sensible format, and here was his chance.

He pulled the pad toward him and drew a line down the middle of the page. At the top of one side he wrote "Income." They wrote down what Deet's mom could expect to make in a month, tips and all, and then he wrote "Outgo" on the other side. They wrote down the monthly payment to the lawyer. That was first, because what would happen to Dad if his lawyer wouldn't work because he hadn't been paid?

They were lucky that they didn't have to pay any rent or house payment, because Deet's dad had built their house. So there was food, and electricity, and fuel oil, and the phone bill, the newspaper, and gas for the car. And there was a payment for a car they didn't even have any more, that red Corvette, and there was a lot of money they had to pay on that stupid charge card. And miscellaneous. There was a lot of that. Mom chewed on the end of her pen and wrote down "stamps" and "clothes" under miscellaneous. Then she added "beauty parlor" and "medicine." Every time she thought she was finished she thought of another miscellaneous. "Oh, cleaning supplies," she said. She wrote it down. "That *must* be everything now."

Mom added up each column on the little calculator, her tongue sticking out like P. J.'s when she was printing something. When they added it up, the Outgo was bigger than the Income.

Mom folded her lips together and squinted helplessly at the figures. At last she said, "Sally said I could write to the credit card company and they'd cut the payments down."

"Wow. That's good," said Deet.

"If I hadn't found a job I could get unemployment,

and Dad could get a free lawyer. Isn't that the strangest thing you ever heard?" She leaned back and took a deep breath. Well, they'd just cut all the extras. She wouldn't go to the beauty parlor, and she'd trim the girls' hair herself. She shot a look over at Deet's hair but shook her head. "No. You'd better go to the barber. Your kind of hair is too hard to cut." Deet was relieved. He remembered the haircuts Mom had given him when he was little. They were pretty weird.

They agreed that they could cut the food bill down by doing without fresh fruit and vegetables and fresh milk. Powdered milk would do it. And now that the worst cold weather was over, they could turn off the furnace and use the woodstove. There was a lot of wood stacked up in the yard. When they'd cut out beauty parlor and fuel oil and a lot of the grocery money, the columns matched and there was even a little left over.

Mom thought a minute and said, "I'll ask the lawyer if he'll let me make smaller payments."

She looked up suddenly. "Grandma called this morning. She asked you to call back."

Deet searched her face. "Did she say anything about Dad? What does she want?"

"Nothing. She didn't say anything. Just said for you to call. Probably has chores for you."

Deet started to write the budget over again on a clean sheet of paper.

"Dad said there are a lot of people in there who have parents who won't have anything to do with them. Sheena's mom and dad won't go see her brother. There's this one woman who was embezzling from somewhere and her mother brings her kids to visit, but the grandma doesn't say much. She looks mad all the time."

Mom laughed. "I've seen them."

"And then there's this old black guy, who looks at his daughter like she was the moon and the stars. Did you ever see him? People sure take trouble in different ways."

Deet frowned at the phone. "Well, I'd better get it over with."

He dialed Grandma's number. "This is Deet," he said when she answered.

"Deet, could you come and give Grandpa a hand with the wood after school tomorrow?"

Deet didn't answer for a minute. Was it supposed to be business as usual after all these weeks? Was Grandma going to pretend that it hadn't happened, that there was no long silence from them?

"No, Grandma," said Deet. "I go to see Dad after school."

There was a silence, and his grandma said, "You go to the *jail*?"

"Yes."

"I think that's awful," Grandma said, in a shocked kind of way. "What are your parents thinking of?"

"Lots of kids go there to see their moms and dads, Grandma. I'm not the only one. And lots of parents go to see their kids, too. Tell Grandpa I'm sorry I can't help him, but Mom's working now, and we're really busy."

When he hung up, Deet felt bad. He suddenly missed Grandma, her little soft face, her quiet ways. He hadn't thought how hurt she must be to have her child go to jail. What did that feel like? Maybe as bad as having a dad go to jail.

Deet's mom was sorting the bills into piles with

yellow sticky notes on top. Pay all now, write a letter, pay a little.

Deet was finally cleared for his first contact visit. You weren't allowed to have a contact visit until all the paperwork had been screened, to see if you were the kind of person who would try to smuggle something to the prisoner. Even if you were just a kid.

The prisoners were searched before they came in, and after the visit they were strip-searched. But still people smuggled in stuff, and sometimes they got caught, and sometimes they got away with it. Dad said it was silly making all that fuss about tobacco. Why didn't they just let them have cigarettes, anyway?

The contact visit room was the room you could see through the window when you went into the regular visiting room. Here twenty prisoners could have visitors. Everyone had to sit on folding chairs placed just so, in view of the cameras. It looked like the kind of semicircle you made in school for music class, except that the director was a guard.

Deet lined up with the other men to be searched

before they were allowed in. He had to take off his shoes and put his hands against the wall while the guard ran his hands up and down his body, patting here and there. The guard shook his shoes and looked them over carefully. The women were being searched behind the lockers. Then they let everybody into the room to wait for the prisoners to be admitted.

Lots of kids were there, running around the contact room. There was an older woman and two very ancient Indian or Eskimo women. There was Meghan and Ian and their grandmother, the fat girl with the baby, and Andy, and there was a black family who were the largest people Deet had ever seen. The woman, the man, and the old mother were all well over six feet tall and not skinny, but wrestler size.

The prisoners came into the room one by one, after their search, and went to sit with their visitors on the folding chairs. There was a lot of hugging and kissing, and noise. When Dad came in he gave Deet a quick hug, which was not the sort of thing that Dad did on a regular basis. Dad looked different up close and without the glass between them. Better, really.

A huge black man was the last one in, and he joyfully embraced everyone in the tall black family. He was bigger than any of his visitors. The four of them were overwhelming, and the most happy-go-lucky bunch you'd ever like to see.

When Della came in, the guard had to remind her and Andy that enough was enough as far as contact was concerned.

The man took his baby on his knee, and he and the fat girl watched him with delight. Meghan and Ian were talking to their mom ninety miles a minute. The grandma sat silent, her mouth in a straight line, her face cold.

Dad leaned closer to Deet. "See that big guy there? That's Big Henry. He gave me a haircut yesterday. He's here for murder."

Deet tried not to stare at the big black guy and his jolly, laughing family. This was what a murderer looked like. This big guy, full of fun and life. He was going to be locked up, maybe forever.

"He killed his father. Said he was the meanest guy who'd ever lived, beat his mom up all the time, beat all the kids, and tried to do it when they were grown up as well. They'll be sending him to a penitentiary here shortly, and he's got a long time to do." Dad was quiet a minute looking at Big Henry. "I was thinking, I lived my whole life without ever knowing anyone I thought should be dead." Deet couldn't think of anyone either.

"Hey, I've got a new room," said Dad. "They moved me out of that cell this morning and I'm in the wing now. It's a lot better. Only two of us to a room, and there's a big dayroom in the center where we can watch TV and stuff."

"Who's in the room with you?" asked Deet.

"He's okay," said Dad. "Interesting to talk to. He robbed a bank."

Deet could picture a guy with a ski mask and a bag full of money, waving a gun around. He couldn't help but smile, but Dad didn't notice.

"I'm going to get a job in the laundry on Monday. Ronny works there. He put in a good word for me. He says it's not a bad job and it'll make the time pass a lot faster, especially with Ronny there. He's always up to something, got something funny going on. He keeps everybody laughing. Only fifty cents an hour, but every little bit helps."

"That's good," said Deet. He frowned, imagining Dad bending over a tub of soapsuds, scrubbing a uniform. Of course that was silly: They'd have washing machines and dryers, wouldn't they?

"Mom brought your report card in for me to see yesterday. The guard even let her bring it into the contact room."

Deet smiled.

"I thought maybe your grades would go down, after all that's been going on. All the work you've been doing at home. That's really good, Deet. I would have felt pretty bad to be the cause of your grades slipping."

A pang of guilt assailed Deet. Actually, he had put a lot less effort into all his work, except for Mr. Hodges's class. Sometimes he didn't even pay much attention in class. He had been very surprised to find that he could get the same grades by doing much less work with much less effort. Maybe he'd been overdoing it all these years.

"I finished that last book you sent me, that one about

the guy with a retarded brother, *Of Mice and Men*. My roommate is reading it now. I knew it was going to end up sad, but I just couldn't stop reading it."

"He wrote a lot of good things," said Deet. "Steinbeck. I could get some more by him."

"My roommate has read a lot," said Dad. "He's a real smart guy, educated. He's already sentenced, waiting to be sent to a federal prison."

"What'd they give him?" asked Deet.

"Ten years," Dad said.

Nelly ate lunch with Deet every day in the cafeteria, and they sat way in the back. And sometimes now Sheena ate with them too, when she didn't have a music lesson.

Nelly didn't ask questions. It seemed to Deet that any other kid would have asked *something,* how long does he have to stay in there, or something. Deet knew that Nelly really liked Dad, liked to hang around when Dad and Nelly's father were fixing a truck in the yard, something Deet didn't really enjoy at all. But Nelly didn't ask anything.

Ever since they'd been in kindergarten, Nelly had

done all the talking. Deet had been quiet all his life, hadn't had much to say to anyone, really, but now he felt like he owed Nelly something.

So one day while they were eating lunch, Deet said, out of nowhere, "Dad's got a job in the laundry now. You know what they pay them? Fifty cents an hour." Nelly gave Deet a startled look, but he didn't say anything, just kept working on his sandwich, which he was having a hard time keeping together, because the part with the lettuce kept slithering away from the part with the tomatoes. "I wish Mom would just give me peanut butter," he grumbled.

Once he started talking about jail, Deet didn't want to stop. He told Nelly about the guy who just wanted a house and a dog, and the bank robber who liked Steinbeck, and all about Ronny.

"Nothing's like you think it's going to be in jail. There's a guy who's a murderer, and he's so nice and jolly he could play Santa Claus. He cuts the guys' hair." Nelly looked fascinated and didn't interrupt, he just nodded. Nelly had a very understanding nod, Deet thought.

When Deet went to visit Dad that day after school, there was a prison van with steel grids behind the driver's seat parked by the front door. The guards were letting the prisoners out, and Deet's stomach went cold when he saw that one of them was Dad. He was handcuffed and there were chains on his leg. He was chained to another prisoner, and they had to sort of shuffle together to get up the stairs and into the jail. Dad didn't see him.

Deet closed his eyes and pressed his forehead against the walls of the prison and waited until he could get himself together.

It was easy to get caught up in the stories, the normalcy of prison, the people and their lives, and then you saw something like this that made you remember what jail was all about.

SIXTEEN

After Deet had put the girls to

bed that night, and had done the dishes and lunches, he went to his room to do his homework.

First he went over the budget he and Mom had worked out. The lawyer had agreed to let Mom make smaller payments, so Deet could change the figures in the Outgo column.

Now that they were concentrating on it, they could find lots of ways to make ends meet. After he'd cleaned out the cupboards, he had figured out that they could skip a week's shopping if he'd fix meals from food that was already in the house and not buy something new. There were boxes of instant meals long forgotten in the backs of the cupboards, noodles with something sauce, Chinese dinners. And there was still some hamburger in the freezer.

There were a lot of things you could make with hamburger, which was about all they could afford in the way of meat. Sally had given him a recipe for meat loaf, which he'd made tonight. Meat loaf, he was surprised to discover, was just meatballs made bigger. Or meatballs were meat loaf made smaller.

Actually, the more he got into this cooking thing, the more he could see that there were only so many basic things to eat. You just arranged them a little differently to get a different result. Like a taco was just a hamburger, really, it was just that the bread was different, and the meat was crumbled up.

Deet did his other homework before he got out his quotations notebook. He'd found a good quotation that morning and he knew he'd have a lot to write.

Distrust all in whom the impulse to punish is powerful. —FRIEDRICH NIETZSCHE

In the morning before school I read the newspaper now, anything that has to do with jails or crimes, or anything like that. I never even

noticed stuff like that before my dad went to jail.

There was an article about how the state legislature wanted to make prisons rougher. Prisoners should have no frills—no television, no educational classes, and most of all, no lobster. The article said that prisoners got a lot of steak and seafood and all kinds of fancy food. How does stuff like that get in the newspapers? I know there aren't any education classes, and there's no music allowed except radio, and most of all, there isn't any lobster or steak. Just turkey.

In the paper there are always letters to the editor from people who are upset because someone didn't get a hard enough sentence at his trial. Or someone who thinks the death penalty is not too much for this crime or that. There are a lot of people like that. That's what Nietzsche called a powerful impulse to punish.

Even kids have a powerful impulse to punish. When someone gets in trouble at school, there are always kids who hope they get the book thrown *at them. Once when we were talking about having a kind of student court, the principal said it wouldn't work because kids were always twice as hard on other kids than the teachers would be. What's that all about?*

Or what about that trial of that guy that blew up that big building, and after, they interviewed people on the radio and TV, and all of them just wanted the guy to fry.

Nobody said, Well, I feel sorry for him. Maybe he was crazy, or maybe he had a terrible life. Nobody thought about what it was like to be the guy. Or his family. It was just kill, kill, kill. Aren't you always supposed to look at both sides of something?

Maybe most people aren't that nice.

The next day at school Deet was reading when Sheena came to sit with him in the cafeteria at lunch.

"Where's Nelly?" she asked.

"He stayed home because his mom was sick. He asked me to get his math assignment."

"My brother had his trial yesterday," Sheena said.

Deet's eyes narrowed. The word "trial" was terrifying. "What happened?"

"He was convicted," she said. "There was never any question about it. He did what they said he did. He robbed someone's house."

"Jeez," said Deet, shocked. "What made him want to do that?" It wasn't as if Sheena's brother had been raised poor, or was a foster child, or abused, like the people Dad talked about. He'd grown up in one of those houses on the ridge.

Sheena just shook her head. "Maybe he wanted to get back at our folks."

Deet looked startled.

"What do you mean?"

Sheena looked at him for a minute, considering. "I don't know how to describe my folks." She ran her fingers over the pile of books she'd put on the table. "They're cold," she said finally.

Deet looked at her, trying to understand what the word meant when you were talking about people. He wasn't sure he'd ever known anyone who could be called cold.

"What do you mean, exactly?" he said.

"Oh, you know. Like they'll pretend to be interested, but it's fake, and they don't want to even make you believe it. They belittle you somehow. They have voices that never get excited. And their faces are like that. Always the same. I don't think they like kids at all."

Grandpa was like that, thought Deet. Except he didn't even pretend to be interested. Mom and Dad, he guessed, must be the opposite of cold. Warm. Alive and loud and funny.

"Do you get along with them?" he asked.

"Not really. But I don't say anything. I just do what they say. I know I'll be grown up in a few years. But Billy would fight them all the way. He called them hypocrites."

Deet scowled, trying to imagine Sheena's life.

"What are *your* folks like?" she asked.

Deet could see one of those Christmas pictures Dad took every year. A little out of focus, but nice just the same. He looked at the table before he answered, afraid he was going to say something stupid.

"I used to think they were like kids, kind of disorganized and all. Well, they *are* like that. But they're good-natured. And happy. And they really like kids."

Sheena looked at him sadly. "I thought so," she said. "Your dad looks so kind." Deet noticed that Sheena's face was smooth and calm, but she hardly ever smiled. Her smile was a widening of the eyes, a tightening around the forehead. Maybe she'd better learn to smile before it was too late.

"How much time did they give him?"

"You have to wait for the sentencing to know that. He'll be sentenced in a month or two."

"Oh, yeah," said Deet. "I forgot. That's a long time to wait to see what's going to happen to you."

He had a sudden suspicion. "You didn't go to the trial, did you?"

"Yeah," she said. "I took the day off from school."

Deet felt ashamed. Sheena was the bravest person he'd ever known. He'd been afraid to go to the jail. He'd never be able to go to Dad's trial.

Deet crumpled up his napkin and thrust it into the paper bag. "What was it like?" he asked, finally.

"They brought him in in handcuffs. And shackles. On his legs."

Deet looked at his bag. "I saw Dad like that too. They were taking him out of the prison van." He tried to get that picture out of his mind as soon as it popped in. "Did your folks—"

"No," Sheena interrupted. "They would never. The worst part was when the lawyer and the judge talked about him as if he was this low, disgusting person. I felt like jumping up and saying, You don't even know him. You don't know how funny and good he can be. You don't know what he was like before."

She looked at Deet with such sorrow that his throat ached.

She stood up and gathered her books together. "See you later," she said.

That afternoon, when he and Sheena were waiting for Rhonda to let them in, they watched two little kids playing jail. "I'm having a contact visit," said one, and the other searched her all over just like a guard.

"Little kids," said Sheena. "Nothing bothers them.

Like kids you see on TV, like in a war zone. Playing around all those tanks and things. Soldiers with guns."

"My sisters," said Deet. "They didn't miss a beat. They miss my dad, but they didn't go into overdrive or anything. All the little kids who come in here to visit are like that. I guess you have to be as old as us to be ashamed." He thought a minute. Of course it helped that no one at school had ever said anything to the girls—little kids probably wouldn't know anything, anyway—and because P. J. and Jam still bought the story about the headlight.

Deet pointed out the old black man who always laughed and joked with his daughter.

"I like his face," said Deet. "George Orwell said at fifty you have the face you deserve." Sheena gave him a look, so he told her about Mr. Hodges's class and the quotations. He showed her his quotations notebook.

Sheena flipped through the pages and finally looked up. "This is so great," she said. "Can I take this and read it?" He looked at her, startled, and she said quickly, "Well, maybe it's too personal. I understand."

"No," said Deet. "No. I'd like to have you read it.

Mr. Hodges writes a lot of neat stuff. He used to work in this jail."

"You write about *jail*?"

"Well, yeah. It's kind of on my mind right now."

"That's so cool. I don't have anyone to talk to about it." She paused a minute. Then she said, "Except you."

Sheena was popular, had always had a lot of friends around her. "What about those girls you hang out with?" Sheena ran her hands through her hair, her face suddenly hard. "They stop talking when I come into the bathroom. Throw little looks at each other, talk in this fakey-sweet voice. They *enjoy* people's troubles." Deet knew how that would be. He was glad he was a loner.

"You know how they have this group for kids whose parents are alcoholics?" said Sheena. "They should have something like that for kids with someone in jail. So they'd have someone to talk to too."

"Yeah," said Deet. It was a good idea.

The visiting room was crowded that day: Meghan and Ian and their grandma, the old couple Deet had seen on the first day, visiting the Eskimo boy, Michael and his mom, the old black man, and Big Henry's enormous family. They were like old friends now to Sheena and Deet.

Dad was looking better these days, now that he'd gone to work. Not so pinched. Deet asked him about the laundry job, and then they talked about the book Dad was reading, *The Grapes of Wrath*. Deet hadn't read it yet. In that book the hero goes to jail for killing someone. Dad thought it was great.

Deet could hardly believe he was talking to Dad about books.

Just before it was time to go, one of the prisoners passing by the back window stopped and waved at Deet. Dad turned around to see what Deet was looking at.

Dad smiled. "That's Ronny," he said to Deet. Ronny mimed shuffling cards for Dad, and Dad gave Ronny the thumbs-up sign. "He's saying we'll have a game of cards before dinner tonight," Dad explained.

Deet stared hard at Ronny, he'd wanted so long to see him. A short guy with curly dark hair falling in his face and a brilliant, happy smile. Ronny waved good-bye and Deet waved back before the guard made

Ronny move past the window. Deet and Dad stared for a minute at the window where Ronny had been, both smiling. It was true what Dad had said. Ronny had a sort of cheering effect on people. Somehow he made you feel good.

"Doesn't he ever have any visitors?"

"Not a one," said Dad.

SEVENTEEN

Some days everything seemed

to go wrong. The washing machine developed a leak and spewed suds all over the floor, the damper on the wood stove was wobbly and nearly smoked them out sometimes, the water pipes had to be thawed with a hair dryer a few times because they didn't know how to baby them the way Dad did when it was cold.

Dad went nearly frantic when things were going wrong at the house, so Deet and his mom agreed that they just wouldn't tell him about any problems that came up. That was hard to do, because they needed to ask questions about how to do this or that, but as soon as they did Dad would nearly jump out of his skin at having to talk about how to do something, instead of just doing it.

But one morning the car wouldn't start. Bingo and

all the guys at the shop had said they'd look after things, just call, but so far Deet and his mom hadn't done that.

First of all, they were kind of ashamed to, because after all, it wasn't as if Dad were sick. And second of all, they knew it would make Dad feel bad if they got the guys to help them, especially if they had to take time out from work.

But Mom had to get to work, and they sure couldn't afford to pay the wrecker to take it to the shop, so Mom called Bingo to come and look at it.

Bingo said he'd be over at noon, so Mom called Sally to ask for a ride to work. Deet decided he'd stay home from school that morning to give Bingo a hand.

When Deet opened the door for Bingo he felt a surge of happiness, just like he was a little kid again, when he'd go to the shop and Bingo would take a candy bar out of his toolbox, or stick him up in a car that was going up on the lift. There was Bingo on the porch, undiminished, carrying his huge toolbox. His very bulk was comforting, all the rings of fat over his belt, the pads of flesh under his eyes. Deet was smiling so hard his cheeks felt funny.

Deet followed Bingo into the kitchen. "Mom said to give you coffee before you started."

"That's a good woman," said Bingo. "She knows how important coffee is."

Bingo hung his parka on one of the hooks by the door, then sat down at the kitchen table. He watched Deet pour the coffee.

"Hey," said Bingo, "we really miss you down at the shop."

"Yeah, I miss coming, too," said Deet.

"Well, this will all be over pretty soon, and things can go back to normal," Bingo said.

"Yeah," said Deet.

"You're looking kind of skinny," said Bingo.

Deet smiled. "Well, I'm doing the cooking now, and I don't eat as much when I cook as when Mom does."

Bingo made a horrified face. "I guess I'd get skinny on my own cooking too! Good thing Mary does all that."

He took a big slug out of his cup and asked for an ashtray. When he'd lit his cigarette he asked, "How's Charley doing?"

"Okay. He's got a job in the laundry."

Bingo brooded over his coffee. "I'd go crazy if they locked me up."

"Maybe it's not as bad as you think."

Bingo made a *yeah, right* face.

"You should see how people laugh and all. It's not like everyone's all miserable and depressed all the time."

"That's just how people are," said Bingo. "When I went to Vietnam I was scared to death at first, and I couldn't get over how everyone else acted. Laughing all the time. It took me a while to figure out they were just as scared as I was. But people anywhere make fun of their situation. Gallows humor, they call it. Guy making jokes on the way to his hanging."

He exhaled noisily and squinted at Deet through the smoke.

"You mad at him?"

No one had asked Deet that before. He felt a jolt of shame, remembering the rage he'd felt when Mom had first told him.

Deet wiped his hands on his pants as if he was

getting rid of that memory. He didn't want to tell the truth, but you couldn't lie to Bingo.

"I was at first. I was ashamed. You know, the papers and all."

Bingo nodded.

"Then I just started feeling sorry for him and scared for him. Like he was going to be in with a lot of bad guys and get beat up and all that. And that was crazy. It's not like that, not like the movies. But what you find out is that it's so easy to get in trouble. Just one day something goes wrong and there you are. Now it seems to me like it could happen to anyone. I know there are some really bad people, you know, people who torture some guy because he's black or gay or something, and Dad says some of the younger guys like to act real tough, but I think most people in jail are just—unlucky, I guess."

Bingo reached over and ruffled Deet's hair, something he hadn't done since Deet was a little kid. "You know, you're an all right kid," he said.

After Bingo had the car up and running, Deet went to his desk and tried to find something in the quotation book that could describe someone like Bingo. He couldn't find exactly what he had in mind, but he found this one:

Most of our misfortunes are more supportable than the comments of our friends upon them.
—CHARLES CALEB COLTON

Lots of times when something bad happens, people say the wrong thing. Things like, Oh well, it could have been worse, or things will look brighter in a few days, or something like that. That's not what you want to hear. You want to hear them say that's the most horrible thing I ever heard of! I don't know how you can stand it.

Or maybe they will lecture you like, you shouldn't have done that, or that was really stupid, or something like that. If you've done something stupid you already know it, and you don't need anyone else telling you that.

But we are really lucky. Most of the things people say to us about Dad being in jail are not like that. Like Bingo, who doesn't try to act like what Dad's going through is nothing, to make you feel better. He says right out that he'd go crazy if he was locked up in jail. You might not think that would make you feel better, but it does, because you know Bingo is really feeling for Dad. Nearly everyone we know is like that. They say the right things.

When Mom got home from seeing Dad on Sunday, she was full of the stuff she'd seen and heard in the jail that day. When Deet thought how she'd hated the place at first, he had to laugh. Now it was her favorite social scene. She had friends, and she knew the stories of nearly all the people who had been there for a while.

She'd done her grocery shopping after she'd visited Dad and was dashing about the kitchen, putting things away while she told him the jail news.

"Ronny got out today. Dad says he'll miss him, but he's really glad for him. He'll be on parole for a year, but he already has a job waiting for him, and he's going to take his little girl out of foster care and start to live like a real person."

"I saw Ronny for the first time the other day," said Deet. "He was walking in the hallway and he stopped to knock on the window at Dad. He's got this big smile."

Deet took the bag of potatoes Mom had bought and dumped them out of their bag into the bin he'd cleaned out for them. He looked to see if there were any bad ones.

"I wonder why no one ever came to visit Ronny," he said.

Mom looked at him thoughtfully, then gave a little shrug. "I don't know."

She took the eggs out of their carton and lined them up in their little wells in the refrigerator door.

"The other news is that they shipped Big Henry out, so we won't see him anymore."

"Where to?"

"Dad didn't know. Some penitentiary where they keep guys who have a long time to serve. I'll miss seeing Big Henry. And his family! They just never stopped laughing. With all this hanging over their heads. Nobody to give haircuts now either."

Mom shoved cans of soup in the cabinet over the sink with the canned fruit. It made Deet crazy to see her mess up his perfect system. He'd put them in the right places when he was cooking dinner. He spent a lot of time walking around behind Mom and P. J. and Jam, cleaning up their mess and disorder.

Mom slammed the last cupboard door and stuffed all the grocery bags into the garbage can. Deet pinched his lips together so he wouldn't remind her that he'd put a special bag in the pantry for the plastic grocery sacks, so they could be recycled. He was trying not to be a nag.

"Dad said he told Ronny to write to him and Ronny laughed and said that would never happen, because he wasn't any better at writing than he was at reading."

"Ronny couldn't read or *write*?"

"Not much, I guess."

"How could *that* happen?" Deet asked, horrified.

"That's what I asked Dad. He said Ronny had gone from one foster home to another, one school to another. It just never clicked with him. Dad said a lot of guys in there could hardly read."

Deet stared at Mom. Not to be able to *read*. How

did people get by without being able to read? What could be worse?

When Deet sat down that night to do his homework, he looked for a quotation about someone who couldn't read. He found one that seemed pretty appropriate.

Better build schoolrooms for the boy than cells and gibbets for the man.—ELIZA COOK

Dad says a lot of people in there can barely read. Schools shouldn't be allowed to let kids get out of school without being able to read, should they? That should be against the law, shouldn't it? It seems to me that maybe if you don't give people a good education, you can count on their getting into trouble. It's one of the saddest things I've found out about jail.

When Deet got his homework back at sixth period the next day, he read what Mr. Hodges had written at the top:

Did you know that the United States puts more

people in jail than any other industrial nation? And did you know that we also have the highest rate of illiteracy in a nation that's not "third world"? You're right about the connection between not being able to read and a life of trouble. Our country has a lot to be ashamed of.

And at the bottom of the page, Mr. Hodges had written:

Here's a quotation for you.

No evil so great but that some good comes of it.
—PLATO

When my mother had cancer, she went to a support group meeting—you know, a lot of people with cancer—and the guy who ran the support group asked them all to talk about the good things that cancer had done for them. They were all shocked to think that anyone could talk about good coming from a disease so horrible, one that could kill you.

That did kill my mother. But then my mom said they all started to think and talk about the good things. One woman said it brought her closer to her kids. And so on. Maybe you'd write something for me about that—the good things this jail experience has done for you, your dad, your family.

Deet thought about that for a long time, and so many things came to mind that he started to make a list.

He printed Plato's quotation neatly at the top of a clean page and began to write.

When you stop and think about it, maybe it was a good thing. Everyone sort of stopped what they were doing and said, maybe we're off course here! Maybe we need to do things differently. I think my dad thinks it was good to get stopped before he'd been taking drugs too long to quit. And he thinks about how he might have hurt someone, driving when he wasn't straight. I like it that my dad started to read, too.

I guess the really good things are what we

learned about people. Well, maybe my mom and dad knew most of it already, but I didn't. There are some people we've known all our lives—the guys Dad works with and our neighbor Sally, who turned out to be really good friends. I never thought about friends before. I thought it just meant people you hang out with. I never thought I had any friends, really.

There's Nelly, who rides the bus with me. I never thought much about Nelly, but he is a real friend. I don't know how to explain it exactly, but it's like he's guarding me. I never knew Nelly would care so much about somebody else's feelings. I'm glad I found that out about Nelly, because to tell you the truth, I never gave him much credit.

And other people, who you thought of as enemies, some of them turned out to be friends too. Like I thought prison guards were all guys who like to shove people around. But there's Mr. Tobolowsky. I don't know how he got to be a guard, but he's just this little skinny guy who sees inside *people. He sees things other people don't think about. Like he told this one woman, "It must be hard to work and take care of a baby and visit here all the time." She just about melted, to think someone would notice. And he talks to me, and to Sheena. He told me what a nice guy my dad was, and I felt like someone had given me a present. Because even though my dad is in jail, someone noticed what he was like, he was a real person to Mr. Tobolowsky. And he asked Sheena how her brother was getting along. He told her he was worried because Billy, her brother, is very depressed. He notices things about people, and he worries about them.*

So that's another good thing I learned, not to dislike someone before you know them.

And we met a lot of people we'd never have met it this hadn't happened, and we've heard a lot of stories. All the stories make us feel lucky. Like before, we never noticed how good we had it. Especially me. I never noticed what great parents I had.

It was late in the afternoon on Easter Sunday when Grandma called again.

"Deet, I have some little things for the girls for Easter. Ask your Mom if I can bring them over."

He should have realized that Grandma wouldn't let a holiday go unnoticed. She was always big on Valentine's Day and Easter and birthdays, things like that, nothing last-minute like Mom. Grandma really put her whole heart into it.

"Mom had to work today, because they get so many people on Easter," he said, "but sure, come on over." Then he remembered that Grandma never drove the car if she didn't have to, especially after dark.

"Is Grandpa coming?" he asked, dreading the answer.

"No," she said brightly. "Just me."

The girls were delighted to see Grandma. She brought chocolate bunnies and her special Easter pastries, huge Easter cards, the kind that cost a lot of money, and lots of packages tied with lavender and yellow ribbon. There was candy for Mom and a shirt for Deet, and each girl had a new outfit.

When the phone rang and P. J. yelled, "It's Dad!" Grandma looked shocked.

"He calls on the phone?"

"Almost every day," Deet explained, "unless they have a lockdown. Then . . ." He stopped in midsentence because he had a feeling Grandma wouldn't want to know about prison routine.

P. J. was chattering away to Dad when Grandma suddenly walked to the phone and said to her, "May I talk to him, please?"

P. J. threw Deet a startled look, then handed the phone to Grandma, who turned her back to them before she began to speak.

"Charley, this is Mom. How are you, son?" Deet and the girls could tell from the sound of her voice that she was crying. She was listening to Dad and trying to get control of herself.

At last she handed the phone back to P. J. and carefully wiped the bottom lids of her eyes with the tip of her broad, wrinkled thumb.

She bustled about, picking up wrapping paper from the rug, not looking at Deet.

"Well," she said, "he sounds all right. It was so noisy in there, just terrible. I could hardly hear him. But he sounds all right."

She pinched her lips together and frowned at Deet.

"He's not the first person who ever got in trouble, you know, Deet."

"Well, yeah, I know that, Grandma."

"Well, your grandfather is a stubborn Finn," she said. "He doesn't know that."

Deet had never known Grandma to speak so firmly before. And he'd never known she had ideas before, never known that she would ever disagree with Grandpa.

She put her parka on. "Tell your mom I'll come again, Deet, and tell her to call on me if she needs any help. And tell her I'm sorry that Grandpa yelled at her."

After she left, and the girls were asleep, Deet added a few more sentences to his list of good things.

My grandma, who was this sort of nonperson, just my grandpa's shadow, came out and kind of defied him. That was a really good thing. I never

knew she had that in her before. I think I used
to make a lot of mistakes about people before this
happened.

The next time Deet went to the jail, Andy sat next to him on the cold metal stools in the visiting room. They were waiting for the guard to let the prisoners in, when the guard on duty picked up the phone opposite Andy and said something to him.

Andy looked shocked. "What?" he said. "Are you sure?"

The guard nodded, looking sympathetic.

Andy turned to Deet. "She's refused to see me," he said, wonderingly. "She told him to tell me she doesn't want to see me anymore."

Andy stared at the wall for a few seconds, then got up and left. "See you," he said.

The guard let in a woman prisoner with a big belly. Pregnant. She sat down opposite her visitor, a guy with a Spanish accent who didn't even say hello but began to argue furiously with her, as if he was continuing an argument from the day before. "You can't give this baby away," he said. The woman on the other side was angry, thrusting her chin out to make a point, her belly pushed against the metal counter. "*I'll* take care of him," the man said. "Listen to me!"

Deet felt sad listening to the man who wanted to take care of his baby, felt sad thinking about the look on Andy's face when he left. The more he saw of people in this jail, the sadder he got about people altogether. And the luckier he felt.

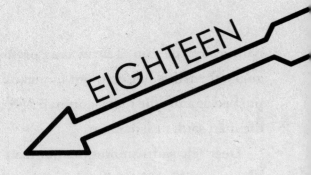

EIGHTEEN

On the day before Dad's trial,

Mom gave Deet a bag of clean clothes to take to the jail, because Dad could wear street clothes when he went in front of the judge the next morning. She wouldn't let Deet go to the trial with her. "Dad doesn't want you to go, and I don't either," she said.

"Sheena went to her brother's trial," said Deet. "She said it was awful, hearing people talk about her brother like he was . . . a criminal." He and Mom smiled at each other, it sounded so funny. Could you believe they were finding something like this funny?

"God, she's brave," said Mom. "I don't think I could have done that at her age."

"Is Dad nervous?"

"He's a wreck," said Mom.

"But remember what the lawyer told you. We know what's going to happen. It's not as if he was pleading not guilty and there was a jury and all. This is just cut and dried. That's what the lawyer said."

"Yes, I know," said Mom, "but what if the judge has had a bad day? What if he's feeling crabby?"

"It's not the trial you have to worry about," said Deet. "It's the sentencing. That's what everyone says. This guy, Andy, was telling me. If you plead guilty there's nothing to the trial, really, but it's the sentencing where things can get crazy."

Deet bent down to straighten up the boots and shoes, which were jumbled together by the door. With his back turned to her, he said, "Mom?"

"What?"

"When Dad went to his hearing, I saw him when they were bringing him back to the jail. He had handcuffs on. And chains on his ankles. He was chained at the ankles to this other guy. That's what they do when they're out of the jail. It's the worst thing I ever saw." He turned to look at her. "You've got to get ready for that."

Mom looked at Deet, horrified. "Oh, my god," she murmured. Deet could see that she was trying to imagine it, but he knew that all the imagining in the world wouldn't show her what men looked like hobbled together, humiliated, chained.

"I'm glad you told me that. I never realized."

Deet was glad Dad wasn't one of the big criminals, like Big Henry or someone like that. With guys like that, big news, there would be reporters and cameras and lots of people at the trial. Dad was just a run-of-the-mill prisoner, no news in him at all. That was good.

Deet called her at noon to see how the trial had gone.

"I had to wait through two trials before his, so I had calmed down a little by the time it was Dad's turn. He looked so . . . I don't know . . . young . . . sitting there by his lawyer. And they didn't give him the clothes you took to him. He was wearing just the stuff he had on when he was arrested. His shirt looked like it had been stuffed into a little bag all this time, all wrinkled and shabby. I could have cried." Mom sounded as if she would burst into tears, just thinking what Dad had looked like. Then she made her voice brighter. "But that's over. *Over.* Now there's just the sentencing to go through."

When Deet visited the jail after school that day, he was almost afraid to ask about the trial, afraid to upset his father. But finally he did. "Was this morning pretty bad?"

"Not so terrible," Dad said. But Deet thought he looked strained and pale, paler than usual.

"The lawyer told me how it would go, and everyone in here tells you what it'll be like, so there weren't any surprises. It's just that you feel so bad. One day you're on the side of law and order, and the next thing you know you're in handcuffs and everyone's sort of not looking at you, you're sort of a piece of business, and no one feels obliged to be courteous or polite to you. You're one of the bad guys." Dad tucked the phone under his chin and then ran his hands slowly down his thighs to the knees, as if his palms were wet.

"I can't believe anyone who's been through this would get in trouble again. I can't believe anyone would do anything that would make them go on trial a second time," he said, his face grim.

So Deet knew that "not so terrible" was not really what Dad thought.

Sheena rode to the jail with Deet on the bus the next afternoon, and she read the latest additions to Deet's quotations notebook.

"This is the last week for the quotations assignment," said Deet. "It was one of the best things I ever had to do in school. I'm sort of hooked on them. Every time something happens, I go look for a quotation. It's like everything in the world has already happened to someone and someone has written about it. Now we're going to do Shakespeare."

Sheena made a face, but Deet said, "Mr. Hodges can make anything interesting."

Rhonda was very fluffy that day, with a bright pink blouse and a full, white, swirly skirt with pink polka dots and high heels with laces that wrapped halfway up her legs. Deet wasn't sure what the look was meant to be. Square dancing?

Andy signed in and came directly to them. He was looking very pleased with himself. He pulled a little velvet box out of his pocket and flipped it open. It held a ring made of some kind of silver metal with a jewel in the center.

"Is it a diamond?" Deet asked, interested. He'd never seen a diamond before.

"Yeah. An engagement ring. Maybe this will put her in a better mood."

"Does she know about it?" Sheena asked.

"No. I'm just going to spring it on her."

Deet frowned, thinking of all the ways this could backfire on Andy. What if Della wouldn't see him again, or what if she didn't like the ring? What if she didn't say the right thing? He didn't want to see Andy get hurt.

Crazy Michael was the only little kid there, and as usual, Michael's mom was running back and forth in the waiting room, trying to keep Michael from banging on the lockers, swinging from the water fountain, trying to climb up the copy machine. Her red sweater was missing some buttons, and she looked pretty frazzled, but little Michael was dressed beautifully, like a little man, with sturdy little laceup boots and a little flannel shirt. You could tell from that how much his mom loved him, Deet thought.

Andy put Michael on his lap and began to play a noisy game with him, and Michael's mom sat down next to Deet with a sigh of relief and said, "I told your mom I hoped Michael would grow up to be just like you. But she tells me you never ran around, you were quiet all your life. So I guess I'm gonna have me a *wild* teenager." Sheena laughed.

Della was the first prisoner the guard let into the visiting room, and Sheena and Deet talked together, trying not to watch when Andy pulled the ring out of his pocket and showed it to her. On the other side of the glass, Della was covering her face with her hands, and then she got up and pressed her lips against the glass. She looked very, very happy with the ring, and Deet and Sheena looked at each other. Sheena had tears in her eyes. Michael's mom and the other visitors were watching Andy and Della, trying not to look as if they were.

The tall, athletic guard was the one who was letting the prisoners into the room. Sheena bent to Deet and said, "He always reminds me of that guy who played Superman in the movie." Deet looked at him again and laughed suddenly. Sheena was right. That's just what he looked like. "He's really nice, isn't he?" said Deet.

"Yeah. My brother says if he catches somebody with cigarettes he just looks away and never turns them in. He's not like some of the other guards."

"No strong impulse to punish," said Deet, and Sheena smiled because she remembered that quotation from Deet's notebook.

A very old prisoner with a cane walked past the windows in the hallway outside the visiting room. He stopped and had a word with the Superman guard, who said something to make him laugh, and then the guard opened the door to let Michael's dad in, and Sheena's brother, and finally Dad. Dad sat down and took the phone and smiled at Sheena. Della twirled on her chair and leaned over to tell Dad about the ring, Deet knew, because she gestured to Andy to show it to

Dad. Dad looked at the ring and smiled at Andy, and then he reached out and gave Della a one-armed hug.

Deet looked that night for quotations about marriage, but he couldn't find one that seemed right for Andy's case. He decided to write about it anyway.

There's this guy who comes in to see his girlfriend in jail every day. He's got a job at the parts counter at the Chevrolet dealer, and he takes his break to visit her. He's been coming a long time, and he knows everybody who comes to visit, practically. He's a calm, easygoing guy, short and stocky, and he's got a lot of thick dark hair and dark eyes that look very kind. He gave his girlfriend a ring today.

I don't think that girl is wife material. I can't see her cooking or taking care of a baby. But maybe that's not what it's about anymore. I don't know exactly what people get married for.

Anyway, Andy, the guy, looks like he could do all of the cooking and baby care, and everything else, too. Maybe some people really like taking care of other people.

The next day Mr. Hodges wrote at the bottom of his paper:

"I don't know what marriage is about either, because I'm not married. Even if I was married, I might not know. We live in confusing times."

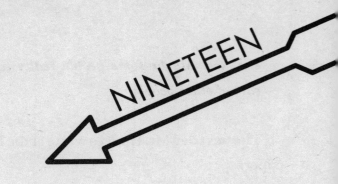

NINETEEN

The night before Deet was to

hand in his last quotations homework, he added to his good things list. Every time he thought he was finished with it, he thought of something else.

I learned I was wrong about a lot of things. I used to think people who had fancy houses, fancy cars, had these perfect lives. But they have to come visit people in jail too.

I used to think that some things were so bad you could never live through them, things that hurt so bad it's like you've been stabbed. But now I think you can live through anything. It just slowly gets easier every day. After a while you can even joke about something that was so terrible at first that it made you want to throw

*up to think about it. That's a good thing to
learn.*

After Deet had visited Dad on Wednesday, he stopped
in the CD place to wait for the bus. The guys had a
scruffy-looking orange cat sitting on the counter. The
cat was not happy to have a big dog nosing around and
batted at him if he got too close.

"Where'd you get the cat?" asked Deet.

"He was just hanging around for a few days, living
under the front step. Look at his ears, tips frozen off.
People should take care of their animals. We call him
Homeless. Know anyone who wants a cat?"

Deet looked into the calm green eyes of the cat and
smoothed his back fur. The cat arched and bumped
his head against Deet's jacket. *People,* thought Deet
sadly. *Don't take care of their kids, don't take care of
their animals.*

Sheena's brother was sentenced and was waiting
transfer to another jail. He was as sullen as ever and
still didn't talk much when Sheena went to see him.

Sheena was having a hard time with the idea of having her brother gone, in some other place where she couldn't visit him. "It's as if this has become my job. And all these people we know. How will we know how everything worked out for everybody?" Deet had never thought of what would happen when it was over. Maybe he'd miss visiting too. And he was sure Mom would. Hard to believe how your attitude could change.

Grandma came to visit the girls once a week now, and she always brought homemade pastries and cookies and huge bags of grapefruit and apples and bunches of bananas. If Dad called while she was there, she talked to him on the phone, and one Sunday she brought Grandpa over.

Grandpa acted as if nothing had ever happened, as if he'd been there just yesterday.

So Deet and Mom acted like that too.

On Friday morning Deet was skimming the newspaper, as he always did before he went to school. When he turned to the second page, the dark print of the head-line on a short story sent a jolt of fear through him:

Somehow Deet knew before he read the story that it was about Ronny.

Ronald Joseph, recently released from the correctional center, was arrested Saturday night after a fight in which Gilbert Aniak, 43, was stabbed with a four-inch hunting knife. The pair had apparently been drinking together in Aniak's apartment when the incident occurred. Aniak was taken to intensive care, and Joseph is in custody.

Deet put his head in his hands. He felt sick, the way he'd felt when Dad was arrested. *Ronny.* You got to know when to hold 'em, know when to fold 'em, know when to walk away and know when to run. His little girl.

When Deet went to visit Dad that afternoon, he saw Ronny being led past the back window, handcuffed. He was wearing red.

TWENTY

After he visited Dad on Friday,

Deet stopped by the used CD place as usual. As soon as he walked in, he knew what he was going to do.

"You still got that cat?"

The young guy with the earring gestured to the top shelf, where the cat was curled up, paws tucked under his chest, eyes closed.

"How about if I take him home?" asked Deet.

"Cool," said the guy. "He needs a good home in the worst way." He looked at Deet carefully. "Sure your mom won't mind?"

Deet hadn't even thought about Mom, but he knew she wouldn't mind. He shook his head. The guy reached up to the shelf, took the cat down, and put him in Deet's arms. "Congratulations, Homeless. You got a home."

"I'm going to call him Ronny," said Deet.

"How come Ronny?"

"Just after a guy I know," said Deet.

When Deet got him home, Ronny sniffed every corner of the house carefully, let himself be petted by the girls, and found a warm corner on the shelf over the washing machine, in a pile of extra towels. Deet put down a bowl of tuna and some milk. Ronny didn't like the milk, but he went mad for the tuna and purred crazily the whole time he was eating. When Mom got home and saw Ronny, she got the same look on her face that she got when someone gave her a baby to hold. Deet could see that Mom really liked cats. She rubbed the cat's chin while Deet told her about the CD guys and all.

"He's been fighting," she said. "See the scar on the back of his neck? And here on his muzzle. He'll have to be fixed, or he'll keep fighting." Deet raised his eyebrows at her. He hadn't known she knew anything about cats, and here she was sounding like some kind of expert.

"We had cats on our farm," she said. "One day my dad got mad and shot them all because he said there were too many." There was a tight line around Mom's mouth when she said that. It was the first time Deet had ever heard her talk about her dad. He had a pretty good idea now why she hadn't wanted to talk about him before.

"Oh, I'm glad to have a cat around again," she said, when the cat closed his eyes and rubbed his jaw against her finger. "What're you going to call him?"

"Ronny," Deet told her. Mom looked at him searchingly, and then she nodded sadly. "Ronny," she said.

Dad was sentenced in early May and was released for the rest of his time not already served to a halfway house. He went back to work, though he had to come back to the halfway house after work. He would be out on parole in another two months.

A lot of the people who had disappeared from the jail over the months were at the halfway house with Dad. The first time Deet visited, he saw the black girl and her dad, and the fat girl with the baby, who could walk now. The sleek-haired Eskimo boy was there too, though someone besides his grandparents, or whoever those old people were, was visiting him. Everyone looked so different out of their prison uniforms.

Visiting was as loose as could be—no searches, and everyone sat in a big room with beat-up couches, a pool table, and Coke machines. It felt like a party to Deet, everybody so relaxed. You didn't notice how tense people were in jail until you saw them in the halfway house.

Deet saw Andy in the supermarket, and he said Della was out of jail and they were getting married at the end of the summer.

Deet had news for Andy: Michael's mom was now working as a cook in the diner where Mom worked. Mom said she was a really good cook, and lots of people came in now for her specialties, like barbecued ribs and what she called her down-home meat loaf.

Deet brought Dad a book every week. You had to give it to the staff member who signed you in, so they could check it for contraband, but at least he didn't have to mail everything he wanted Dad to have. He'd read another of Deet's favorites, *All Quiet on the Western Front*.

Dad had had a letter from his roommate, the bank robber, who'd been sent to the States to a federal prison, and he said it wasn't so bad there. But he was homesick and missed his wife and kids. And his dog. Ronny had been sent to another prison too, but Dad had Ronny's address, and he sent magazines to him every month. Not much he could do for Ronny, he said, but he could do that.

"Whatever happened to the guy who just wanted a house and a dog?" asked Deet.

"I don't know," said Dad. "I'd sure like to believe he got them. But people get in the habit of screwing up, and they just can't break it."

"Like Ronny," said Deet.

Dad looked at Deet with the sorrowful expression he always had when he thought of Ronny. "Yeah," Dad said. "Like Ronny."

Sheena's brother was sent to the prison near Anchorage. She wrote to him twice a week. Deet wondered what she found to write to him about, when he'd been so hard to talk to.

"Well, I write like you did for Mr. Hodges," she said.

"I just write down anything I think about anything, and that can fill up a long letter. Maybe none of it will be interesting to him, but I don't want him to be alone in the world."

"Does he write back?"

Sheena smiled, a real smile, not just her face-tightening thing. "I just got a letter from him yesterday. And he wrote what he thought about everything I wrote. It was like having a real conversation with him, and not like any I ever had with him before. He's like a different person when he writes. Isn't that funny?" She smiled at Deet. "And I sent him a quote book, too. I hope he enjoys it as much as you did."

Deet took Ronny the cat to the vet to have him neutered, and the vet gave him some special food to make up for the long period of malnutrition. After a few months Ronny's coat was sleek and glossy, and he purred all the time. Not the usual cat purr, but some kind of jerky, erratic, loud noise, more like an engine breaking down. It always made people laugh when they heard him the first time. Ronny especially liked Sheena.

Mom said that she'd gotten used to working again and she liked her job, so she was going to work for a while longer, to finish paying the lawyer's bills. Deet said he didn't mind doing the housework and cooking and that he didn't mind taking care of the girls in the afternoon when Mom was at work. He could go to the garage in the mornings now that school was out for the summer, and he and the girls could ride their bikes to the library. They'd stick to the budget that Mom and Deet had made up so that they'd get the credit card paid off. And they'd never go into debt again.

Mr. Hodges sent a postcard from the Rockies, where he'd gone on a canoe trip. He didn't write anything, just drew a picture of himself in a canoe, paddling like mad and looking terrified.

Sheena came to the house a few afternoons a week, and she helped Deet bake brownies and things he hadn't tried to cook yet. The girls were pleased to have her there, a big girl, even when she wouldn't play Barbies with them. In fact, when Sheena told them she thought Barbies were stupid, the girls stopped playing with them so much. Mom always asked Sheena to eat dinner with them when she was there on the weekends, and Deet liked to hear the two of them in the kitchen together, laughing. It seemed to Deet that Mom had taught Sheena to laugh.

Sometimes when it was raining they called Nelly to come over. He taught them to play poker, which was a lot of fun, and sometimes they played Monopoly. The first time Deet got the card that said, "Go directly to jail. Do not pass go. Do not collect $200," he and Sheena looked at each other, but it didn't hurt like it used to.

They knew jail wasn't funny, and maybe they would always wince when people made a joke of it, but they were a lot tougher than they used to be.

Jail wasn't the end of the world.

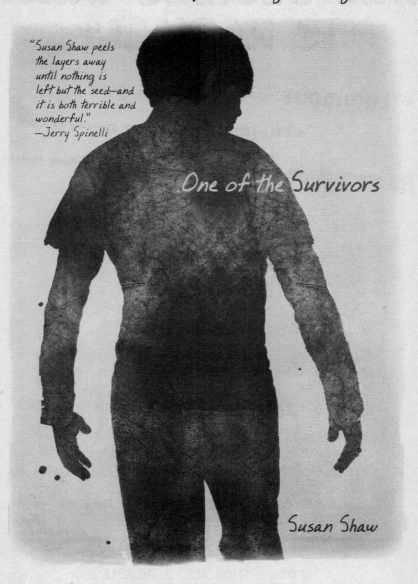

The fire was only the beginning....

"Susan Shaw peels the layers away until nothing is left but the seed—and it is both terrible and wonderful."
—Jerry Spinelli

One of the Survivors

Susan Shaw

Read all the NEWBERY MEDAL Winners from Atheneum!

THE HIGHER
POWER OF
LUCKY
by Susan Patron

KIRA-KIRA
by Cynthia Kadohata

SHILOH
by Phyllis Reynolds
Naylor

DICEY'S SONG
by Cynthia Voigt

FROM THE
MIXED-UP FILES
OF MRS. BASIL E.
FRANKWEILER
by E. L. Konigsburg

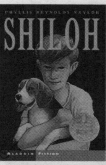

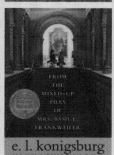

THE VIEW FROM
SATURDAY
by E. L. Konigsburg

MRS. FRISBY
AND THE RATS
OF NIMH
by Robert C. O'Brien

THE SLAVE
DANCER
by Paula Fox

PUBLISHED BY SIMON & SCHUSTER